WHEN THE STARS DANCE

BY ROBYN ANAKIN VEARY

BOOK ONE IN THE TRUE ORDER SERIES

To Nathalie and Michelle,
for their belief in my work

To Jeanne,
for her insight

And to my mother and father,
ever encouraging, ever loving,
this is for you

Table of Contents

WHEN THE
STARS
DANCE

THE FIRST IN
THE TRUE ORDER SERIES

PART ONE:

SIGHT

Chapter

ONE

It was pitch black. Whether his eyes were open or closed, it seemed to make no difference. He tried it a few times: opening his eyes, closing his eyes, opening his eyes, closing his eyes, open, close, open, close. No difference. Strange. He let out a sigh and tried to focus on other things. What he could tell for certain was that he was lying on his back on a soft surface, what he thought could be a mattress. He prodded it with his hands, and yes, it definitely felt like a mattress.

He sat up. A squeak emanated from below what was definitely a mattress and vibrated through it. He assumed the mattress was placed on top of a steel bed frame; that was the sort of noise he imagined it would make. There were no other noises, he noted with a frown. He swung his legs over the edge of the mattress. When his feet met the floor, he saw a thin sliver of light creeping in from under what he assumed was a door. The light was just enough for him to make out the outline of the shoes he was wearing. Still frowning, he stood up and attempted to examine himself further in the dim light. He was wearing a long overcoat, a shirt and long pants, all black. The clothing fitted him perfectly.

It occurred to him that he had no recollection of these items of clothing or ever having put them on. He looked around for some sort of clue as to what was going on. He did not remember the small room he found himself in, or how he had gotten there or, now that he thought about it, what his name was. There was nothing in the room besides the bed, and that was no help.

Static noise sounded painfully in his head for a split second but then was replaced by thoughts and images of a woman he did not know. She was old, kind-looking, but filled with sorrow. He wanted to help her, wanted to do everything in his power to end her suffering. Abruptly, the images and feelings associated with them disappeared and he was left alone in silence again.

He took a few deep breaths, trying to order his mind. He realised that standing in the dark room would not bring him answers. He turned to the door. Feeling around for the handle, he found it and hurriedly pulled it open.

Chapter

Two

He was standing in a long, thin corridor, bathed in light.

Once his eyes had adjusted, he looked to his left and saw there were many doors on either side of the corridor. The red carpet on the floor looked worn. The walls were beige, with light fittings on one side of the corridor after every few doors. He turned right. There were three doors on either side of the corridor before it ended in a T-junction. He turned and looked back into the room he had just been in. He could now see that the bed took up one half of the room and that there was also a tall locker in the other corner he had not been able to see before.

It was still very quiet.

As he pulled the door shut, he saw there was a number on it: 187. He was not sure what it meant, so he tucked it away in his mind and walked down the corridor. When he got to the T-junction, he looked to his right. More corridor with more doors and more lights. To the left, there were only two doors on either side and then the corridor ended.

The carpet was replaced with large reflective off-white tiles and lots more light. Curious, he walked towards it and found himself in what looked like the foyer of a fancy hotel.

The foyer was vast, with a high embossed ceiling where three large chandeliers hung. Along the wall to his right, there were six or seven elevator doors, same as the adjacent wall and the one opposite. Directly across from him was the beginning of another corridor. In the middle of the room, there were a number of circular couches.

He realised that it was quiet too. The only sound he heard was a shuffle of movement to his left. He turned towards the sound and saw a long counter at the end of the room. It was high, about chest height, and made from a dark wood. There were three people behind the counter. A man at the far end was leaning over the counter, holding up his fist and repeatedly drumming the air with the index finger of his other hand. The man's mouth was moving but he couldn't hear what the man was saying. The only visible part of the person in the middle, a brunette woman, was her head. Her hand came into view as she slapped it down on the counter in front of her face, tapped it a few times with a finger and then offered the air a clenched fist. She dropped her hand and nodded, looked up again, and she too began speaking soundlessly. It was still perfectly silent, he realised, and he wondered what the noise was that he had heard.

Then his eyes were drawn to the third person, the one closest to him. She was staring at him, arms crossed, and she seemed to be leaning on something. She offered a smile and waved, as if calling him over. He looked around to see if it was meant for him. He saw no one else, so she *had to* be waving at him. He cautiously began to move towards her, taking deep breaths. As he got closer to her, he could see that she had red hair, tied up behind her head, and light blue eyes. Her smile seemed genuine, he thought. This calmed his nerves slightly, making one corner of his mouth twitch into a half-smile.

As he reached the counter, she dropped her arms and took a few steps forward, right up to the inside of the counter.

"Hey Cormac," she greeted cheerfully. "I'm glad to see you're up. We were beginning to worry you wouldn't complete your transition. *But,* you clearly have. How ya feeling?"

Cormac? Was *that* his name? It sounded right. And what did she mean by 'transition'?

"Still kinda out of it, huh?" she probed. "Don't worry, Cormac, it'll come to you soon enough." She smiled knowingly. "You'll see."

A look of realisation flashed across her face, and with an audible sigh, she busied herself with scratching around under the countertop, first here, then next to it, then next to that. Cormac looked towards the other two. The woman in the middle was hunched over what he could now see was a desk below the countertop, one clenched hand moving furiously over the desk. The man walked through a doorway, concealed by filing cabinets, and disappeared.

"Ah, here we are!"

Cormac jumped, turning his attention back to the red-head.

She had the fingers of her left hand pinched together, as if she was holding on to something, and waved her hand about triumphantly. She took the other hand and held it in the same way as the other but a slight distance apart. Her eyes moved between the two hands, then she looked up at Cormac again.

"You've received your charge, yes?"

Cormac was still stuck on 'transition'. He did feel out of it.

"Mrs Williams has been waiting for this moment for the last six years, ever since her husband transitioned. The poor thing." The woman sighed, looking down at the space between her hands again. She shook her head, looked back to Cormac, and smiled. "Never mind. What'll happen is you'll visit her three times in those six years, and you'll collect her on your third visit. Understand?"

Cormac looked at her with a blank expression, head cocked slightly to one side. Mrs Williams must have been the old lady he had seen in his head when he was in the dark room. All right, that was one thing he understood. The rest …

The woman laughed. "You're a little confused and that's okay. You'll figure it out as you go."

"Go where?"

"Oh, so you *can* speak," the woman laughed. "I was beginning to wonder, though Ahreesey swore she heard you screaming before your awakening. Anyway, you're gonna go visit Mrs Williams – Joyce – and get to know her. She's a lovely lady—" she checked her hands again "—and she'll treat you well as your first charge. Just remember though, transitioning is a delicate topic for the breathers, so go easy on her."

Transitioning … Cormac suspected he knew what that was now. Dying. But *he* had transitioned. So, had he died?

"How do I know where to go?" Cormac asked, changing tack to keep his mind from exploding.

"You take that first elevator on the left," she said, pointing towards the metal doors. She grinned at him and nodded her head. "You'll figure it out."

Cormac felt like that was all she was going to give him for now, so he looked around for a moment, then back at the woman, and gave her a small smile. "Thanks," he muttered, nervously tapping his fingers on the counter, and turned to walk away.

"Oh, and Cormac?"

"Yeah," he breathed, turning back to her.

"Come find me after your first visit. I'll show you around."

"Thanks, Jiëlle."

She nodded and smiled.

Cormac walked towards the elevator. It was only when he reached the doors that he realised that the woman behind the counter had not told him her name. Yet she had not corrected him either. Was he right? Was her name really Jiëlle? It had to be. But how could he know that? Must have been the same way he had known that the old lady in his head was Mrs Joyce Williams, the person he was now going to see.

As he stretched out a hand to press the call button for the elevator, he realised that there wasn't one. He looked in the direction of each elevator and saw that none of them had buttons or markings or any directions. *How strange,* he thought. Before he could turn to call Jiëlle and ask, the doors in front of him opened. Cormac stood there for a moment, looking into the empty box, then stepped inside and watched the doors close.

CHAPTER

THREE

CORMAC STOOD OUTSIDE a house.

There was a low wall around the large house and its garden, and as he looked around at the other houses on the street, he saw that all of them had similar low walls. *This must be a safe place to live in*, he thought. Looking back at the house, Cormac tried to remember how he had gotten there. Strangely, he couldn't. Perhaps losing chunks of time was a side-effect of that transitioning thing that Jiëlle had mentioned. That was just another on a long list of strange things he had gone through in the last ... well, since he had woken up. And then there was the matter of him probably being dead. But how could he be dead and walking around like this? It made no sense. And if he had been alive before this, why didn't he remember anything from that life?

Someone bumped into him.

"Sorry," a tall, large man said, as he and a sniffling, petite woman walked past and almost into him as they walked down the pathway to the house. Cormac watched them for a moment. They were both dressed smartly in black. When they got to the doorstep and rang the bell, a small boy jerked the door open and invited them in. He looked about seven or eight and was wearing a suit jacket and a bow-tie that was too big for his small neck.

Cormac stood for a moment longer in the warmth of the day. A smile came to his face, and he closed his eyes, dropping his head to one side. When he opened his eyes, a newspaper on the ground caught his eye. Picking it up, Cormac read the date. It meant nothing to him.

"Excuse me," a voice called from behind him.

Cormac turned around and had to look down to see its owner. It emanated from a small, old lady in a black dress with a small hat on her head.

"Are you here for Charlie's wake?" she enquired.

Cormac nodded.

"Very good," she answered. "You can take me in."

She took his arm and leaned on him, as she directed him down the path towards the house. Cormac tucked the newspaper under his arm and obliged.

It was a two-storey house with large windows on either side of the front door. The garden was quite extensive; there were small shrubs lining the pathway to the house, and many flowerbeds dotted all over. *It's a very pretty house*, Cormac thought. The lady's voice broke through his reflections.

"My husband is ill at the moment," she told him.

"I'm sorry to hear that," he said, confused as to why she would share such information.

"Yes, thank you," she replied. "He would have been here to help me, you see, but, alas."

"And now the pleasure is all mine," he smiled at her. "I'm Cormac."

"Lovely to meet you, Cormac. I am Joanne." After a second's pause, she added, "Did you know Charlie well?"

They reached the front door, and Cormac rang the bell.

"Not really. I'm here to see Joyce, actually."

"Me too. She's my sister, you know."

The door was pulled open with some force but not by the small boy who answered the door before, as Cormac had expected, but by a tall, blonde, young woman. Immediately, he noticed the antique broach that she was wearing, which seemed out of place with her black dress.

"Hello, Hanna," Joanne said, letting go of Cormac's arm and reaching up to hug the much taller Hanna.

"Hi, Jojo," Hanna said, bending her knees and hunching over to hug the old lady better. "Thanks for coming."

"How is she doing?" Joanne craned her neck to try and see inside.

"I'm not sure." Hanna glanced over her shoulder too. "She's not said a word since she sat down in Gramps's chair. But Nina reckons that Erica's the one to bring her out of it. You know how close they are."

"Well, perhaps her older sister can help too."

Hanna rubbed Joanne's arm and stepped aside for her to pass. She chuckled quietly to herself and shook her head as she began to close the door. Cormac cleared his throat. She looked at him, her smile fading quickly, then she waved him inside.

"Um ... thank you," he muttered as he passed her.

Just inside of the entrance hall, Cormac stood for a moment, watching the people. Hanna joined him a moment later. The living room was full of people, all dressed in muted tones. They were milling about, drinking tea or coffee or eating snacks, and looking sad and sombre. The only sounds were those of cups being clinked against saucers and the respectfully soft murmur of voices. Cormac realised he was rocking on the balls of his feet, so he nodded at Hanna and began strolling about.

Cormac walked around the large room. All around were groups of people, talking solemnly. After a few minutes, he spotted Hanna joining two young women and an older one. He instantly recognised the older one as Joyce. Then he realised that Hanna and the two young women looked very similar, like sisters. The first was sitting on Joyce's right-hand side, holding her hand and stroking it affectionately. She had a bright pink streak in her otherwise blonde hair. This woman looked at Joyce with concern, then to the woman to her other side. This one's long, dark hair set her apart from her sisters.

Hanna knelt in front of Joyce. "Was it nice seeing Aunty Jojo, Gran?" She held out a cup of tea. Joyce's eyes were red and puffy, and she was staring vacantly at the floor. She didn't even seem to notice the tea, or Hanna, or Hanna's sister stroking her hand, or anything else going on around her. Hanna looked up at her sister.

"Just leave it, I think, Han," said the woman with the pink streak.

Hanna nodded and put the cup down on the side table. She put a hand on Joyce's knee and said, "I've put your tea next to you, Gran. It's right here." She gestured towards the table, but there was still no response.

Hanna stood up, an odd expression on her face. She took her dark-haired sister's hand and pulled her aside. Cormac moved through a group of people and stood close by.

"I don't know what to do with myself, Nina," Hanna said, looking over to the two they had left. "I need to do something though, you know? Keep myself busy. Otherwise ..." Tears began to well up in her eyes.

Nina hugged Hanna, resting her cheek on Hanna's head. "Let's leave Erica to it," Nina suggested. She let Hanna go and looked at Joyce and Erica. "She was always closest to Gran. And you and I can do the rounds. You know, talk to people, say thanks for their awkward condolences."

Hanna groaned. "I don't want to talk to these people again. I don't even know most of them."

Nina looked down for a moment, then nodded her head. "I'll fetch my guitar, you set yourself up by the piano, and we'll keep ourselves busy, okay?"

Hanna nodded. The two sisters hugged again before they disappeared around a corner. Cormac turned his gaze to Erica and Joyce. He took a few steps towards where they were sitting, Erica still stroking Joyce's hand. She was definitely Joyce Williams. She was the woman he had had flashes of when he was in the dark room. She was seated on a tatty, worn reclining seat. The broach that she had on seemed to match Hanna's, he noted with a smile.

Cormac knelt down in front of Joyce. As he took her hand from Erica, the sound of music drifted into the room. Cormac focused on Joyce. He leaned down so that his face was in her line of sight.

"Hello Joyce," he said softly. He reached a hand up to her face and wiped a tear that had been hanging from her cheek.

Cormac took hold of her other hand and put them together, cupping them between his own. "Joyce," he said, his tone as before, lifting her chin gently with his index finger and thumb, "would you like some tea?"

She slowly shifted her gaze to look at Cormac and nodded her head. Cormac reached for the teacup and placed it in her hands. She lifted the cup to her mouth and took a small sip.

"Go on," he encouraged.

She took another sip. And another.

Joyce looked at Cormac again, her dark brown eyes meeting his. They stayed like that for a moment. Neither of them seemed to notice Erica jumping up or rushing off or the melodic sounds of the piano and guitar abruptly stopping.

"Would you like to go for a walk?" Cormac asked. He was unsure why he asked, but it seemed the right thing to do.

When she spoke, her voice sounded strained, like she had not used it for a while after overexertion. "I would like that," she muttered.

Cormac nodded his head and gave her hands a squeeze. He stood up, still holding onto her hands, and helped her up. The sisters hurriedly joined them.

"Gran! You're up!" Hanna said with delight.

Nina was smiling broadly.

Joyce nodded, linking her arm into Cormac's. "I'm going for a walk with Cormac. We'll be back soon."

"But Gramgram, who is he?"

"It's great, Erica," Nina stressed.

"He is my second cousin on my mother's side's second husband's first son from his first marriage's roommate from when they were at university."

The sisters shared a confused look.

"Now, lovelies, please excuse us."

Chapter

Four

"I WAS NINETEEN," Joyce continued.

The two had walked arm-in-arm out of what Joyce had called her estate. There didn't seem to be many people about; there were few cars that passed them and fewer people on foot.

Joyce continued, "I was young and impressionable, and Charlie was a dashing young man in a uniform. He seemed so much older and wiser, even though he was only three years older than me."

Joyce giggled quietly and shook her head, just as Hanna had done earlier.

After a moment, Cormac commented, "Hanna seems to be a lot like you."

"What? Oh, Hanna. Yes, yes, I suppose she is."

Cormac could not tell if she had been surprised by his comment or if she had never thought of it before. Looking ahead, he added, "I only say so because she laughed earlier just like you did."

"Truthfully, she is more like her dear mother." There was a hint of sadness in her voice.

"Something happen to her?"

"Mmm." She nodded her head. "Cancer."

"Sorry to hear that."

"Thank you."

It was a warm day, though there was a chilly breeze that swooped by every now and then. They walked in silence for a little while. They had found their way to a small park, walked through it, and reached a road. Cormac looked down at Joyce, her arm still linked in his. Her head was cast down.

"But you were telling me about you and Charlie?"

Joyce looked up at Cormac and smiled. "I was, wasn't I? Yes, where was I?"

"You were nineteen; he was three years older and in uniform."

"Yes!" she exclaimed. "From the moment I met him, I knew he was someone I wanted to know. He had a way of … of by simply being with me, making me feel like the singularly most-important person in the world. He would open doors for me, warn me about puddles, carry my bags for me when he walked me home. Charlie met me three times a week just to walk me home. He would ask me questions about what I'd learnt in class that day or what I had had for lunch or what I thought about the war. Always about me. He wanted to know all about me."

The more she talked about Charlie, the taller she stood, Cormac discovered with a smile. The road they were walking along turned sharply to the left, and they crossed to the other side.

Softly, almost inaudibly, Joyce added, "I was the same with him, always wanting to know everything about him."

Cormac grinned. "That's lovely."

Joyce smiled up at him. "Do you have an important lady in your life?"

He smiled back at her and chortled.

They came to a circle in an intersection and made to cross it. A loud hooting pierced the air, accompanied by the screeching of tyres, as a car skidded towards them. Cormac froze for a second as a flood of images crashed down on his mind: a car, a door that was swinging, a beautiful woman on a swing, shattered glass sprinkled on a tarred road, a woman's scream, screeching tyres mixed with the sound of breaking glass. Feelings of intense pain gripped him as he felt a clenching in his chest, his knee-caps exploding, his shoulder dislocating, his head smashing against the ground, and the candle of his life being snuffed out.

Joyce squeezed Cormac's arm with surprising ferocity. He found himself back in the present and able to move. Cormac flung himself towards her, throwing them both to the ground on the sidewalk, Joyce on top of him.

Cormac had his eyes shut tightly. The hooting had stopped now. The sound of tyres screeched past them, and a man's voice shouted something, then disappeared with the sound of the car. A weight was lifted from his extended arm, and Cormac could hear Joyce's voice.

"Cormac? Are you all right?"

There were more images flashing like a strobe light in his head: a bar counter, twelve or so empty bottles viewed from the side, misting breath, hugging an exquisite girl, pointing and laughing at something across a street with two other men.

"Cormac?"

Joyce's voice was soothing to the panic that had gripped his chest and constricted his lungs. What was he seeing? What was he feeling? Joy, silliness, a sense of adventure? But from where? And when? He did not remember these people or recognise these places.

"Cormac."

Joyce grabbed the hand that had been holding his chest.

"Cormac."

Her touch was soothing too.

"Open your eyes."

Slowly, he did as he was told and looked up at the kind old lady, kneeling beside him.

"There's a good boy. Now, sit up." She tried to heave Cormac up. "Sit up." She groaned as she attempted to help him sit up. "There you are. Isn't that better?"

He felt dizzy and quite nauseous. Cormac looked at Joyce. "Um ... I think so."

Chapter

Five

Cormac and Joyce walked back to the house in silence, once again with her arm in his. They walked a different route, a quieter one with no roads, only footpaths. Joyce glanced up at the tall man, a question on her face, but she said nothing.

Cormac looked at her, his face less pale than before. "I don't know," he breathed.

"Hmm?" Joyce gazed up at him.

"I don't know what happened back there."

Joyce nodded slowly.

Cormac stared ahead when he spoke again. "It's the first time that something like that has happened to me."

She nodded again. She seemed to be uncertain though.

Silence fell again for several minutes. Cormac was not focused on where they were walking; his feet were simply carrying him forwards. Joyce squeezed his arm and gave him a reassuring smile. He returned the smile, but it faded quickly.

After a few more steps, Cormac muttered, "I saw flashes of things, things I don't remember seeing before. It was like … I don't know how to describe it …" he looked imploringly at Joyce.

She made no response, only changed direction and led Cormac down a gravel path. It was narrow, only just wide enough for the two to walk down it side-by-side. Cormac didn't mind the quiet, finding it comfortable to be with Joyce. She let go of his arm suddenly. He looked up and saw that she was reaching for a metal-framed gate. He helped her pull it open. It made a screech as it moved and jerked closed behind them.

Joyce took Cormac's arm again and led him on. They were in a small space; two tall trees stood guard, each in a corner of the semi-circle garden. Joyce lead him to the curving wall and Cormac could see more clearly now that there were small, rectangular plaques evenly spaced along the wall. Cormac felt a sombreness about the place and soon realised why. There was a larger plaque above all the others that read 'MEMORIAL WALL'. He felt the weight of the place, the respect that those who had created it held for those that were commemorated here.

Joyce indicated a plaque on the wall, around the middle of the wall and less weathered than the rest.

"This is where my husband wanted to be placed." Her voice was remarkably stable. "It's been a week since he passed away, but every night in my dreams, he has visited me. We walk and talk … like we used to. He reassures me of how much he loves me and how beautiful he still thinks I am."

Joyce dropped her arm and faced Cormac. "And every night, you join us too. My Charlie greets you like a long-lost friend, and he hugs you. He introduces you, and as soon as I turn to shake your hand, Charlie disappears. I panic, but you take my hand and ask if I would like to go for a walk, just like you did this morning.

"I don't know who you are, Cormac, but I do know that I trust you instinctively. The dreams I had about you didn't make sense until you walked me out of the house, and perhaps their true purpose is still to be seen. Give the images you saw some time. I'm certain they will eventually make sense too."

Cormac wrapped his arms gently around the petite lady and held her close for a moment.

When he released her, he smiled at her. "Shall we get you home?"

Joyce smiled and nodded. "That would be lovely, thank you."

Chapter

Six

It was only once the elevator doors opened before him that Cormac realised where he was.

He took a few steps, and he was back in the foyer. There were three new people at the counter, none of them Jiëlle. He decided to go ask one of them where he could find her. He had questions for her, about what had happened with Joyce and the things he had seen. Perhaps she would know what was going on, or if she didn't, maybe she could tell him who would be able to answer his questions. He needed answers.

He started to walk towards the long counter. Suddenly, Cormac thought he saw, out of the corner of his eye, a grey mass move past him. He whirled towards it, but it was gone. He turned towards the counter again, dismissing it as a figment of his imagination, but right in front of him, another blur passed, like thick smoke on a breeze.

He jumped back, blinked, and it vanished. He looked around the large room; no one was there but him and the three other people behind the counter. The elevator he had just stepped out of opened again. A blur came out of it and headed straight for him. He shot backwards onto a couch, eyes wide, and watched it move towards the counter.

A hand touched his shoulder. He leapt off the couch and spun around.

"Hey, whoow, relax, it's just me," Jiëlle said, holding up her hands defensively.

"But ... wha..." Cormac tried.

"What are you seeing, Cormac?" She glanced around her nonchalantly.

"I ... I ... I don't know ..." His eyes were still wide, his heart beating in his throat. Another stream of grey floated behind Jiëlle.

"You've just returned from seeing your charge?" Jiëlle asked calmly, crossing her arms.

Cormac stared at her dumbly.

"And it went well? You formed a connection that doesn't make sense to either of you?"

He nodded his head slowly, struggling to figure out where this was going.

"They will become clearer," she concluded with a shrug. "Come on." She turned and walked towards a corridor. Haplessly, Cormac followed.

"We all see them differently in the beginning." She spoke so casually that Cormac wondered if she really knew what the eerie blurs were.

They walked straight down a corridor for a while and passed many doors with numbers on them.

"It was only after my third visit to my first charge that I started to see them. And, for me, they were shimmers of light."

They turned a corner and stopped in front of a door with no number on it.

"How do you see them?" she asked, looking up at him.

"Grey smoky things," he answered reluctantly.

She nodded and smiled, while pushing the door open. He followed her inside the room. It was large, with many round tables, a few chairs at each. Against the far wall was one long, rectangular table with many mugs on it. On the wall above this table was a range of differently coloured taps, evenly spaced out in an almost polka-dotted fashion. There were easily over thirty taps. There were also three big couches where half a dozen people were sitting and talking, steaming mugs in their hands.

Jiëlle, untying her thick, long hair, led Cormac to the long table and handed him a mug.

Cormac saw that the taps were not only different colours but also different shapes and designs.

"Pick one," Jiëlle instructed.

Cormac chose the tap right in front of him, one with rounded handles, its blue paint chipping in places to reveal a different blue underneath. He put his mug under the tap and opened it. A thick golden liquid poured out slowly. When the mug was full, he closed the tap and stared at the contents of the mug. He was only mildly aware that the people on the couches had stopped talking and were now watching him.

Jiëlle moved next to him, a dark green broth in her mug that bubbled and spat unappetisingly. She nudged him towards the couches with her shoulder and walked past him. She sat on the arm of one of the couches and addressed the group. "Hey, everyone, Cormac just returned from his first visit."

"How exciting!" exclaimed a woman with short, curly hair. Cormac knew, somehow, that her name was Orkid. "How'd it go?" She made space for him next to her.

Cormac gave a weak smile and sat down. He thought for a moment. "It went well," he replied slowly. "Joyce was very ... uh ..."

"Receptive?" offered Inade, a tall, dark-haired woman, sitting opposite him.

Cormac nodded. He was still uncertain as to how he knew their names.

The man sitting on his other side, with short thick dreadlocks, named Akael, patted him on the back. "It will get easier after this first one, my man," he said, smiling broadly.

"How cryptic, Kael!" chuckled a slim man sitting on the couch next to Akael. His name was Caster, Cormac instantly knew. But how? "He's already freaked out enough without your enigmatic comments."

Akael barked out a laugh. "I'm sorry, my man."

"Akael is right," Inade piped up again, "everything will become clearer after you've helped your first charge transition and with time."

"Can you answer me one question though?" Cormac asked, looking at the group.

"Sure we can," said Rowné, who was sitting next to Inade. He was a big man with a warm smile. "What would you like to know?"

Cormac stared at the golden liquid in his mug for a moment, one immediate issue playing on his mind. "What were those things I saw? In the big room?" He looked up at Jiëlle. "You said you saw them differently to me?"

The group stopped, smiles disappeared, and all turned to Jiëlle.

"He's seen them already?" Eddley asked from her seat next to Caster. Her eyebrows were tightly pinched together.

"That is very quick," Orkid said, nodding in agreement to Eddley.

"You saw them the soonest of anyone, Jiëlle," Akael pointed out, looking at the red-headed woman, "and *that* was unusual."

"Come on, guys, it's not like it's a bad thing," Jiëlle answered with a shrug. "It's just a thing. I spoke to Ludis 'bout it when it happened to me, and he said that it *has* happened before, so it's *nothing* to worry about. Cormac seeing them sooner, sure, it's *really* soon, but it's not anything to worry 'bout either, okay?"

The group was silent for a moment.

Orkid spoke first. "If our intrepid leader said so, well, then it must be so."

There was a murmur of agreement from the group. Cormac watched them, still confused.

"Ludis *would* know," Caster concurred.

Jiëlle smiled at Cormac. "As I said, Cormac, the things you saw will take shape soon enough, so don't stress 'til then, okay?"

Cormac was still uncertain, but he nodded nonetheless.

"Aren't you hungry?" Inade asked.

Cormac once again looked into the mug in his hands. It was still full. He lifted the mug to his nose and smelt it. It smelt delicious. He had not realised until he had taken a sniff how hungry he was. He took a big gulp and, as it poured down his throat, felt a warmth begin to wash over him. It spread to his fingers, his toes, carrying a calmness that flowed through him.

"That's better, isn't it?" Inade asked with a soft smile.

Cormac smiled back at her and nodded his head stupidly.

"This is where we get our sustenance," she told him, standing up. "Breather food is fine, but this gives us the energy we need to do what we do."

Cormac's smile faded. "And what do we do?" he asked.

Everyone laughed and began to get up, heading in their own direction.

Akael stopped and added, "You'll get there, my man." As he walked towards the door, Cormac could still hear him chuckling.

"Aren't you sleepy?" Inade put a hand on his shoulder and rubbed it gently.

Only when the question was asked did Cormac realise that he was. He nodded his head slowly and returned her smile.

"Of course you are," Inade murmured. She looked up and added, "Jiëlle, don't you think you should take Cormac to his room?"

Jiëlle jumped to her feet. "Yes! We could all do with some rest." Jiëlle took Cormac's mug and put it on the table with her own drained one. "Let's go," she said.

Compliantly, Cormac stood up and followed Jiëlle out of the room.

CHAPTER

SEVEN

WHEN CORMAC WOKE up, he was back in the small room he had first found himself in. He remembered how confused he was then, but now he felt at ease and refreshed. There was a soft glow above his head. He looked up and saw that a small light was attached to the side of the locker, which he had not seen before. The light made things better too. He lay on the comfortable bed for a moment and thought about everything that had happened since that first moment he found himself in this room.

The first thing that came to mind was the flashes of Joyce he had had. He thought about her, and he wanted to see her, see how she was doing. Then, he remembered what Jiëlle had said, that he would visit Joyce three times before she transitioned. Cormac wondered if he should find Jiëlle and ask her more about transitioning. His concern for Joyce outweighed his curiosity, so he decided to go visit Joyce first.

He sat up and rubbed the sleep from his eyes. He felt better than when he had woken up here before. He pulled his boots on, which he had thrown onto the ground before sleeping. He straightened the pillow and blanket that were on the bed. When he was done, he smiled, thinking how much nicer this addition made the space feel. He looked around the room, which was feeling more like it belonged to him, then remembered the locker.

He opened it and looked inside. There were three compartments, the one at the bottom was tall enough for an extra pair of boots; an extra set of clothes hung neatly on hangers in the middle, long compartment; and, in the thin top one, there was a small box. He picked it up and examined it. It was a simple, brown-wood box with simple carvings on its sides and on top was the number 187, the same as on the door. He replaced it without opening it and closed the locker. All he wanted to do right now was to see Joyce.

Cormac pulled the door to his room open and stepped out into ... not where he expected. He was in a different corridor, one with dark-wooden floors and walls, and it led straight ahead of him. He stared at the dimly lit space, absently letting go of the door. Where was he? The click of the door closing behind him drew his attention to it. There was no number on it but rather a sign that read 'MENS'. He heard the distant sound of laughter.

Cormac took a step forward, then another, feeling how intensely he was frowning. As he listened and slowly moved along the passageway, he also heard the sound of clinking glasses and cutlery on crockery, talking, and the distant sound of traffic.

The end of the corridor made a sharp right turn and then opened into a long room. There was a bar all along the one wall and the opposite was completely open. In the open space between, there were many tables and chairs, at which some people were seated, eating, drinking, talking. Through the open wall, the fresh air gently drifted in. Outside, in the warm sunshine, there was a long table that caught Cormac's eye. There were about a dozen people sitting around the table, and there, at the head, sat Joyce with a pointed birthday party hat on her head.

Cormac weaved between the tables, heading towards her. As he stepped outside, one by one, the three granddaughters sitting around Joyce all turned to look at him. Cormac didn't notice them though; he went to stand beside the woman he had so badly wanted to see. He put his hand on her shoulder. Joyce looked up and a gentle smile spread across her face.

As Joyce began to stand up, Erica, who was sitting to Joyce's right, jumped up and pulled her chair out.

"Hello Joyce," Cormac said softly, leaning down to hug her.

"Hello Cormac," Joyce replied. She added in a whisper, "I knew you would be here."

He hugged her back and smiled. "I would not miss this for the world."

Hanna, seated on Joyce's left, was now standing too. "Gran?" she asked, stressing the name to show her displeasure.

Joyce stepped back and looked down the table. "Where are my manners?" she giggled. "Everyone, this is Cormac."

Nina waved her hand above her head as she uttered, "Your second cousin's roommate's blah blah blah?"

"Exactly." Joyce smiled at her granddaughter as Erica helped Joyce to sit down again.

"Is he joining us, Gramgram?" Erica asked, not looking at Cormac.

"If I may?" Cormac looked at Joyce.

"Of course you must," she said. "Hanna, be a dear and fetch another chair please."

It was plain on Hanna's face that she didn't want him to join them, but she dutifully did as she was asked. Hanna moved her own chair closer to her grandmother's and put his chair on her other side.

"Here you go," Hanna said, indicating the chair.

Cormac smiled at the young woman and sat down. "Thank you," he acknowledged softly.

He looked around the table. It was filled with people of all ages, men and women, and all were talking to those around them, laughing occasionally, and being generally happy. But suddenly, all sound seemed to vanish as he saw the woman sitting next to him. It did not seem to matter anymore who was there. As his eyes met hers, everyone around them faded away. Her dark-brown eyes drew him in. There was no one there but the two of them. He realised she was smiling at him, and he could not help but smile back.

34

Part Two:

Contact

Chapter

"I said, 'Do I have something on my face'?"

Cormac was lost in her eyes. He let himself fall deep into their depths as he stared. He felt safe, secure, content, comforted like he never had before, not even by the golden liquid. As she spoke, her voice washed over him and embraced him warmly. When she repeated herself, however, Cormac realised what she had said and felt something else that he had not experienced before: embarrassment.

He quickly looked away as he felt his face get hot.

"Is that a yes?" she gasped and grabbed Cormac's arm, whirling to face Nina sitting across from her with a grin on her face. "Nins, tell me it isn't true!" she squealed, almost giggling.

Nina looked at the woman for a moment, smirked at Cormac briefly, then set down her glass, her face very stern. She leaned forwards and looked at the young woman's face.

"Now that he mentions it," Nina said slowly, "you do have something just there." Nina tapped the end of her nose.

The woman gasped again and slapped Cormac's arm. "Why didn't you tell me sooner?" She scooped up a napkin and furiously rubbed her nose. Her brow was furrowed as she looked at Nina.

Cormac's eyes were wide as he looked from the one to the other. What was going on?

Nina bit her lips together, then burst out laughing. The woman sitting next to Cormac also started laughing. Hanna looked past Cormac to them.

"What's so funny?" Hanna asked.

Cormac shrugged, now completely confused.

"Leave them, my dear," Joyce cooed, "they're enjoying themselves."

Nina looked at her sister, still laughing as she spoke, "Anele was just introducing herself to Cormac."

Hanna looked around Cormac again, frowning deeply. "Behave, Anele," she chastised in an angry whisper, "This is my gran's birthday party."

Anele chuckled and looked down, feigning shame. "I'm sorry, Joyce. I didn't mean to enjoy myself."

Joyce's soft, gentle laughter filled the air. She took Hanna's hand and gave it a gentle squeeze. "You should bring Anele over more often, my dear. She makes everyone laugh."

Hanna smiled back at her grandmother and nodded her head.

Joyce turned back to speak to Erica and the woman next to her. Cormac didn't hear what they were talking about because he was listening to what was going on behind him. Hanna had leaned back in her chair and reached behind him. She hit Anele on the arm.

Anele leaned back too. "What was that for?"

"You know what!" Hanna insisted.

"Oh, Han, you need to lighten up. Your gran is fine, and look, she's enjoying herself."

"That's not what I mean, and you know it."

Cormac didn't hear any more because Nina cleared her throat and stood up. The man on her left stood up too. "Everyone," she called, "we'd like to make a quick announcement."

"News?" Joyce asked, taking her hat off.

"Yes, Gran," the man said, putting his arm around Nina's back. "Go on," he whispered to her.

The dark-haired woman smiled and looked up and down the table. "Andrew and I wanted to wait until everyone was together to tell you all that ... we're pregnant!"

There was a joyous outcry from everyone at the table. The men stood up and shook Andrew's hand; the women hugged and kissed Nina. Many were saying how excited they were for the happy couple. Joyce got a kiss from Anele and a hug as she laughed about Joyce becoming a great-grandmother. Joyce laughed too.

Cormac watched the family and remained seated. Eventually, everyone began to mingle, changing seats and talking to different people. The lady Cormac had met outside Joyce's house, Joanne, was there too. She greeted him fondly and introduced her husband, Isaac. The two spoke with Cormac for a little while and then the cake came out.

Anele gave Cormac a piece of cake and then went to sit with Hanna at the other end of the table. Cormac moved up a seat to sit next to Joyce. He commented on how nice the cake was.

"Celeste made it for me," Joyce said. "When she married the girls' father, there were some concerns."

"Concerns?" he asked.

"Well," Joyce began, setting her spoon down, "the first issue that the girls had was that she is closer to their age than their father's."

Cormac looked at the young woman at the end of the table, talking with two people around Joyce's age. *That must be her*, he thought.

"And she's a baker," Joyce added.

"What's wrong with that?"

"She didn't have any money when they met, so the girls ... and I, we all were concerned that she was only with Herman for his money."

"Wasn't that the case?" he probed.

"Not at all!" she smiled. "Her bakery is doing very well now. *And* she did it all by herself. We're all very proud of her."

Joyce and Cormac sat a while in silence, eating their cake. Cormac looked at Hanna and Anele at the end of the table. They were excitedly talking with Celeste. Celeste kept touching the man next to her on the arm. That must be the Herman Joyce had mentioned, the sisters' father.

"They make each other happy," Joyce added abruptly. "That's what matters."

"Are you happy, Joyce?" Cormac looked at her, his concern creasing on his forehead.

A sadness crossed her face for a second but then was replaced with a smile. "It is difficult being without Charlie, but I am surrounded by my friends and family and that keeps me going."

Cormac took her hand and gave it a squeeze. He didn't know what else to do, but as he had seen her do it to Hanna, it must be a comfort. They spoke a while longer, mostly about how Joyce had moved to a smaller house and the new friends she had made there. Cormac noticed that she smiled more as she spoke about the new people in her life.

"What about Anele?" Cormac asked, trying not to sound overly interested.

"Hanna is studying at *Tuks*, and she met Anele there," Joyce explained. "They have been inseparable since the day they met. And she is lovely."

Cormac looked to where Anele was. "She certainly is ..." he breathed.

Anele was standing now, hugging people. Joanne and Isaac and the older couple that had been talking with Celeste walked towards Joyce. She introduced them all to Cormac. The man was Joyce and Joanne's younger brother, Graham, and Edith, his wife. They seemed nice. Edith told Joyce that she was getting tired and asked if it would be all right if they left soon. Joyce, always accommodating of everyone, it seemed, agreed and gathered her things. She walked around the table, said her farewells, then returned to Cormac.

He stood as she approached.

"Thank you," she whispered as they hugged.

"For what?"

"For joining us. For being here. For the strength that you've given me."

He was thrown by this. He had not realised his presence had been so helpful. He gave her a little squeeze and whispered back, "You are stronger than you know. Stay strong."

Cormac waved them goodbye and sat down again, wondering why he had said that. He knew that the next time he would see her would be her last moments, but he was uncertain of when that would be for her. Perhaps she needed that strength to get her through until then? Slowly, he returned to his half-eaten piece of cake. *Might it be soon for her*, he wondered. How many would feel her loss? And after? Where would she go then? He would take her by the hand and lead her away but to where? Would it be a better place? The only person he could think to ask was Jiëlle, and he would—

"You okay?" a tender voice intruded his thoughts.

Cormac looked up and got a bit of a fright when he saw someone sitting in Joyce's chair. It was Anele, smiling at him, and this didn't help him relax; his stomach turned and made him feel uncomfortable, and he could hear his heart beating.

"Hmm?" was all he could manage. Then he realised that she had asked a question, so he swallowed his heart back down and answered, shaking his thoughts away, "Yeah, fine, thanks."

"Where'd you go?" she asked, picking up Cormac's spoon and taking a bite of his cake.

Cormac stared at the woman. Her dark eyes were bright with curiosity, her smile was warm and infectious. He could not help but smile back as she took another bite of his piece of cake.

"You seemed so far away," she added, "so I just wondered where you'd gone."

"I was thinking about Joyce and what she's been through since I last saw her," he answered, while busying himself looking for another spoon.

Anele held out the spoon she had used, but right at that moment, Cormac found another and showed it to her. Anele chuckled and took another spoonful.

She waved the spoonful in front of her as she spoke again. "I've known her for as long as I've known Han, and I think she's wonderful!" she said, matter-of-factly, then she gulped down the spoonful of cake.

There was a roar of laughter from the other end of the table. Cormac looked at them and then back to the beautiful woman sitting next to him.

"Why aren't you sitting there?" He tried to sound nonchalant.

Anele sat up straight. "Do you want me to go?" she asked, giving him a scrutinising look.

"No!" he answered too quickly.

She chuckled softly. He avoided looking at her.

"I just don't want you to miss out on ..." Cormac paused, then, inclining his head towards the others, he concluded, "on that."

Anele cut the last small piece of cake into half and took the smaller bite. Her eyes went to the end of the table, and she shook her head.

"They'll be fine without me," she informed him, giving him a big smile.

This time, it was his stomach that jumped into his throat. He attempted to smile back and swallow it down. Why was he feeling like this? Why had his palms gone all sweaty?

"Besides," Anele added, "I see them all the time. Han and I share a flat, and she's really close with her sisters, so I see them basically every other day. Their dad works a lot, so we don't see him that often, but his wife comes over every time she has something new she wants us to try. It annoys Han sometimes, but I love it … I might have a problem with sweet foods." She chortled with her last comment, and her smile radiated joy in the light of the afternoon sun.

Cormac looked at his last little bit of cake. He pushed it towards Anele with a small smile. "Here," he said softly.

"Are you sure?" she asked.

Cormac nodded, his smile glued to his face.

"Thanks!" she said and touched his arm. She scooped the bite into her mouth and gave him a big smile. Where she had touched him, his skin was tingling. It was possibly the best feeling he had ever felt. His face became hot again, he could almost feel his cheeks fill with colour. He quickly looked away.

At the other end of the table, the baker Celeste was watching her husband as he spoke. Her eyes were fixed on him, like there was nothing else in the world. Cormac looked back to Anele with a small smile. She was speaking to a waiter that Cormac had not realised was there. The waiter walked off and promptly returned with a plate and two cake forks. He placed it in front of Anele and then went to the other end of the table.

"This is my favourite thing in all the world," Anele informed Cormac. "My grandma and I used to make it together when I was little."

She handed Cormac one of the forks, a smile on her face, then picked up her own and took a bite.

"No one makes it like she did," she said with a mouth full of food. She swallowed and added, "But this is still really good."

Cormac looked at the dessert. He did not know what it was, but it did look delicious. Before he could take a bite though, someone gently put a hand on his shoulder. It was the woman who had been sitting next to Erica.

She looked at the two for a moment, and then said, "Sorry, am I interrupting?"

"No, no, Aleiah," Anele smiled. "What's up?"

"We're getting coffee now," Aleiah informed them. Her voice was quiet, shy almost, "and then we're sending Herman home, and well, the rest of us are talking about going for a drink at Papa Joe's. Do ... do you two want to join?"

"Of course we do," Anele answered for them both. Cormac did not mind; it meant spending more time with Anele.

"Great," she smiled and patted Cormac's shoulder. "Do you want me to get you anything else?" Then she added hastily, "besides coffee?"

"Just coffee will be fine, thanks, Alei," Anele smiled. She gave Cormac a quick look, he nodded, then she added, "For us both."

Aleiah nodded and then returned to the other end of the table. Cormac watched her absently as she walked, thinking that she almost seemed to glide. And then they were left alone again.

Anele took another bite of the dessert, swallowed, and then asked, "Have you ever been to Papa Joe's? The one on Lynnwood Road, not the one in Hatfield."

If he had, he was not sure. He only remembered from when he woke up in his room and, the way he was experiencing time, that could have been a few hours ago or a day or two. He really couldn't tell. More importantly, he couldn't tell Anele that. He had his doubts about how well that information would be received. So, he shook his head.

"It's a great place," she beamed. "The prices are reasonable, the vibe is relaxed, proper pub feels, you know. And if we're lucky, Papa Joe will be there too." She took another bite but then a look of sadness washed over her face. "I used to go there with some friends but ..."

She stopped abruptly when the waiter arrived. She thanked him, and they drank their coffee. It was a strange liquid that was simultaneously salty and sweet and left a funny taste in his mouth. Cormac didn't finish it before they left.

CHAPTER

TWO

PAPA JOE'S RESTAURANT and Pub was a large place: they walked through three or four rooms before they got to the one that Erica was looking for. It was a big room, with couches and low coffee tables between them. The group sat by the fireplace where three couches were set around a square table. A waitress came and took their orders as they sat down.

Anele sat in the middle of one of the couches and pulled Cormac down next to her. Hanna sat on her other side. The two friends whispered for a moment, then laughed.

Erica, who sat opposite them, spoke to the group. "It's been ages since we've been here."

Aleiah took Erica's hand as she sat next to her, and added, "I wonder if Joe's here."

Nina, getting comfortable by leaning against her husband, shook her head. "I don't think he will be. From what we've heard, Joe has moved to the other one he opened, so I think that his son is running this one." She looked at her husband, questioning what she had said.

Andrew nodded. "Giovanni, maybe?"

"You mean Gianni?" Aleiah asked.

Andrew snapped his fingers. "That's the one."

"He went to school with me," Aleiah added, "two years ahead of me. He was always that clever one that didn't speak much."

The waitress arrived with their drinks. Anele handed Cormac a large cold glass of golden liquid. She clinked her glass against his and then took a sip. Cormac looked at the liquid in his glass. It looked so much like what he had in that common room with Jiëlle, and the others like him. He hesitated, wondering if it was the same thick goodness.

"Drink up," Anele commanded happily.

Cormac lifted the glass to his lips and let the coolness slide down his throat. It was not the same, he realised quickly, as it cooled him down from the inside. All at once, searing pain convulsed his body and squeezed his head as images bombarded his mind: laughter, shattering glass, golden liquid foaming on the floor, two men holding his arms, a red dress, a flood of confidence, a rug being pulled out from underneath him, landing on the floor, a blackout.

When it was over, all was still for a moment. All was quiet. Cormac blinked, trying to pull some sense out of the images he had just seen. What had he seen?

What was going on with him?

His eyes slowly came into focus, and he saw that there were people standing around him. Anele was kneeling next to him, holding his hand. Her forehead creased with concern, her mouth moving.

What was she saying?

It took a moment longer for his ears to stop ringing, for the sound of a car hooter to go away. Anele's voice was the first thing he heard.

"Cormac? Cormac! What's wrong?"

"Bring a bucket, quickly!"

"Have we picked up all the glass?"

"He only had one sip, Nina, he's hardly drunk."

"Cormac?" Anele's voice drowned out everyone else's for a moment. "Can you hear me?"

"His eyes are open."

"What happened?"

"Did he have a fit?"

"Should we call a doctor?"

Cormac groaned as he realised he was lying on the floor. As he tried to sit up, there were many hands that helped, but the only ones that he noticed were Anele's. Her hands were still holding his.

"Careful, careful," someone said as they helped him back onto the couch.

Cormac's head was pounding. His mouth was dry. Every muscle in his body hurt. This time the memories, if they even were that, were much more intense than previously. He could still feel the emotions all at the same time – the confidence, the elation, the disappointment of something not working out. Everything was rushing through his brain, so loud and so vivid. What was it? What was happening to him? He only knew one person that could help him: Jiëlle.

Pushing through the pain, Cormac forced his eyes to focus. Anele was still kneeling by him and holding his hand.

"What happened, Cormac?" she asked softly.

"I have to go," he said. He tried to push himself up, but she pushed him back down.

"Go where?" she asked, her voice tight. "You can't go anywhere like this."

He thought quickly. "To the bathroom." A splash of water on his face wouldn't be the worst thing.

"Andrew will go with you." It was Nina who spoke now. He hadn't seen her standing next to Anele. She looked towards her husband who nodded and stepped forwards.

He helped Cormac stand, taking him firmly under the arm, and led him to the bathroom.

Once there, Cormac thanked him and walked to the basin. He opened the tap, watching Andrew furtively in the mirror, and splashed water on his face. Andrew handed him a handful of paper towels.

"I have a cousin who has epilepsy," Andrew said as Cormac took the towels. "He found out when he was young, but if this is the onset, then you should definitely have it checked out."

Cormac dried his face and nodded. "I will," he said, amazed at how croaky his voice sounded. He coughed, then added, "I'm going to go to the toilet, so I'll meet you back where we're sitting." He needed some quiet and some time to think, but he didn't want Andrew hanging about, waiting for him.

"Don't worry about it," Andrew said, "I'll wait." He shot Cormac a quick smile, then leaned against one of the basins.

Cormac nodded slowly and looked around the bathroom. There were a few urinals and two stalls. Not sure of where else to go, he headed into one of the stalls and closed the door behind him. He sat down on the closed toilet and thought for a moment.

He had to leave. His head was still swimming with confusion about the … Were they memories? And the feelings that went with them? He had no recollection of ever having felt these things before. Cormac was now convinced he would have to find his way back to … to wherever the place was and find Jiëlle and get some answers. But how?

"Hey, Cormac, you all right in there?" Andrew's voice called from outside the stall.

"Yeah, just give me a moment."

Cormac had to think of something, some reason that would make sense and convince everyone that he was, in fact, okay to leave. But what? He wasn't sure, but he knew he would have to think of something. So, he stood up and flushed the toilet, to keep up appearances. He rubbed his face, thinking ahead to what he would ask Jiëlle, and pulled the door open.

Chapter

Three

He was once again not where he thought he would be.

He hadn't stepped out into the pub's bathroom but in a corridor back where he had started this strange journey. What about Anele and the rest of them? What would they find when they went to look for him? An empty stall and no explanation, no doubt. He tried hard not to think about them ... about her; for now, he had to focus on finding out what was happening to him. He had to find Jiëlle.

Almost as though thinking of it made it happen, Jiëlle walked out of the door in front of him. She jumped back a little when she saw him.

"Cormac?" she asked, looking up and down the corridor. "What are you doing here?"

"I need to ask you some questions."

She studied his face for a moment, sighed, and opened the door she had just come through. She took a step back and waved him inside, offering a tight smile.

Jiëlle's room was slightly different to his own. She had the same bed and locker that he did, but she had nice bedding, a small lamp on a desk next to the locker, and a carpet on the floor. She even had a chair. This was where she sat, leaning forward, resting her elbows on her knees. She pointed at the bed for him to sit, so he did.

For a long moment, neither spoke. Eventually, Jiëlle leaned back, crossed her arms, and asked, "So, what's up?"

Cormac took a deep breath, thinking about where to start. His eyes darted from one thing to another in the room. It was odd that the room looked so similar and yet so different.

"Well?" she pushed. "I do actually have other things to do, you know. I wasn't expecting you back for another few hours."

"I've … uh …" he began, still uncertain where to begin. "I've been seeing things …" he said eventually, "in my head … at random times. Things I've never seen before. Things I … I don't know, but they hurt and … and …"

Jiëlle stared at him, eyes narrowed, forehead furrowed. When she spoke again, her tone was puzzled. "What sort of … *things*?" she emphasised the word he had used.

"I don't know. Things! Pictures of objects and people and places that … that I've never seen before."

Her eyes flew wide open, and she stood up. "Cormac," she said forcefully, "think carefully: what exactly did you see?"

Cormac stared up at her. What was she worried about? Would his answer mean there was something wrong with him? Because that's what he was most worried about. He looked down and thought about the things he had seen.

"I'm not sure," he began.

"*Think!*" she demanded angrily.

"There were bottles and a bar counter and …" and then he was outside, but could he be sure it was him? "… and then there was a road and some other guys and a girl and then ..."

Jiëlle moved the chair closer and sat down again. She edged a little closer still, her face still darkened with worry. "And then?"

"And then nothing."

She leaned back in the chair and looked up. She took a deep breath and let it out. Then she stood up again, pushing the chair backwards, and began pacing around the small room.

"When did this start?" she asked, not looking at him.

"The first time I went out," he answered, watching her walk.

"And it happened again this last time?"

"But worse."

"Did your charge wig out?"

"She wasn't there."

"Why not?"

"She'd left."

"So, why didn't you come back?"

"I don't know. I got invited out by her family."

Jiëlle stopped pacing. Slowly, she turned around to face Cormac.

"Why ...?" It seemed difficult for her to find the words she was looking for. Her teeth were clenched, and her face was changing colour, into one that almost matched her hair.

"It seemed like a good idea." Was he not allowed to do other things with other people besides his charge? She hadn't told him he wasn't. She hadn't given him the rules or 'dos and don'ts' or any direction at all. Did she expect him to guess these things? "Look," he said as forcefully as he could, "it happened before when I was with my charge, and no, she didn't *'wig out'*, as you put it. She was concerned. That's all."

Jiëlle studied Cormac's face for a moment. She seemed to be making up her mind about something.

"All righty," she smiled, her anger suddenly absent. "That's no problem, Cormac. Would you mind coming with me?"

"Where to?" Cormac was on his feet now.

"To the only person that I know that can give you the answers you're looking for." She gave him a sweet smile.

"Okay." He was hesitant, wary of this sudden change in Jiëlle, but what else could he do?

She left through the door and went down a corridor, with Cormac close on her heels. They turned a few corners, and the next thing that he knew, they were in the foyer. It was different now, though. It was full of activity. There were more eerie blurs floating this way and that, and people going about their business. Actual breathers, with arms and legs and heads! Breathers from all walks of life. They were clearly not like him because they were dressed so differently, and each was different from the next.

As he watched a woman walked past him, she faded into a grey mass for a second, then back into a person. Cormac stopped, dumbfounded, and stared. There were queues of people and blurs by the counter, blurs and people talking like there was no difference between them. The four people behind the counter were holding up what looked like pieces of paper, with ever-changing swirls on them, but as he focused on them, those faded too, and it seemed like they were merely holding up their fists. Peering around, he saw that there were groups by the elevators too. Some waiting, some standing with other people like him, people dressed in black whose names he knew. He noticed Rowné standing with a half blur-half man, shaking his hand and laughing.

Cormac felt like he couldn't breathe. *Are the blurs actually people that I can't see?* he wondered. But that didn't make any sense. Why couldn't Jiëlle and the others tell him that that's what they were? It didn't seem that much of a surprise. But the fact that they didn't tell him made him feel like there was more to it, something he hadn't grasped yet. There was clearly something he was missing, some secret, some inside joke he was being excluded from. That is what made him panic. If it was something darker and more nefarious that he couldn't be told about it, how bad could it be?

A hand grasped his wrist.

Cormac looked down to the hand, then up the arm to the face of the person holding him. It was Inade.

"Come on!" she whispered, eyes darting to Jiëlle.

Where she had come from, Cormac could not say, but he listened to her all the same. Not that she gave him much of a choice; she didn't let go of his wrist. They dodged through people and blurs alike as they headed away from where Jiëlle was walking to.

"The blurs," Cormac eventually breathed, "they're people, aren't they?"

Inade stopped abruptly and looked around the foyer. "You see them already? As people?"

Cormac nodded his head. Everything in him was swimming in confusion, doubt, and anxiety that he couldn't find any more words.

Inade made a face, one that was hard to read, and then continued dragging him on. She lead him towards the counter and then behind it. The four people there watched them go past for a brief moment. Inade smiled at them, gave them a wave, then pulled Cormac through a door that was hidden in the corner. One returned the wave, then all turned back to what they had been doing.

"Where are we going?" Cormac asked, finally finding his voice.

"Shh."

She took him through the door, into a room filled with desks and filing cabinets, through another door on the other side, and into a corridor. This corridor was different from the corridors he had been in before. For one, there were no doors along the walls. There were portraits on the one wall, and on the other, there were whiteboards filled with swirling patterns that Cormac couldn't make sense of. They half-ran along the corridor until they got to the end. There was no door there either, only a flat, white wall.

"What now?" Cormac whispered. Why he whispered, he could not have explained if asked.

"Shh."

Again, the monosyllabic answer hushed him, but his mind was loudly racing with possibilities. Was she saving him from some terrible fate if he had gone with Jiëlle? Or was she leading him into a trap, into a fate *worse* than death?

Inade stretched out her free hand and placed it in the centre of the wall. A *'click'* sounded from inside the wall, and a panel popped out with buttons and more of the same, strange patterns on it that he had seen on the whiteboards. She tapped a few of the buttons, all the while edging around so that Cormac couldn't see. The wall turned a bright luminescent green for a second, then it began to slowly swing inwards on invisible hinges. She dragged him inside and pushed the wall closed behind them.

Cormac stood and stared. The room they were now in was perfectly white and of average size – not too big and not too small – and seemed perfectly square. There were two chairs that faced each other in the middle of the room that were as white as everything else. The white walls were bare and even the carpet on the floor was the same perfect white. He heard from behind him another *'click'*. When he turned around to look at the wall, which was actually a door, it was gone, leaving them standing in stark contrast in their black attire to the white room.

"Where are we?" he asked, looking at Inade. As the sound of his voice came out of his mouth, he noticed how his voice didn't carry. It sounded flat, almost trapped inside his ears.

Inade clapped her hands. He heard the clap, but it didn't echo like he expected it to. She walked towards the chairs. "Sound is different here," she said and clapped her hands again. Still no echo, no reverberation, just flat noise. "Everything is different here. Time doesn't even move normally here. I know it's a little confusing, but this is a safe place where you and I can talk openly."

Cormac watched her as she lowered herself onto the chair facing him. Her voice sounded wrong, almost painful to hear.

"Are we still where we were?" he asked, moving around the room.

"This room is technically nowhere, but for all intents and purposes, it's connected to the Told main building through that door." She indicated the chair in front of her, crossed her legs, and linked her fingers together across her lap. She was clearly waiting for him and seemed willing to wait for as long as it took. She offered a small smile, perhaps to try and ease the difficulty of the conversation that they were about to have. "I created this room for just this sort of occasion."

"And what occasion is *this* exactly?" he asked.

"We have things to talk about," she began. "Please," and indicated the chair in front of her again and gave a slight nod towards it.

Slowly, Cormac moved towards the chair and sat down.

"What do you want to talk about?" He tried to appear nonchalant by leaning back.

"Let's start from the beginning, shall we? You asked before what we do here. Have you worked it out yet?" she asked.

"We help people … um, transition," he offered. He wasn't sure if that was the answer she was looking for, but that's as much as he knew for sure.

"That is true," Inade nodded, the palms of her hands spread apart while her fingers stayed locked together. "But what does that mean?"

Cormac swallowed. "We help them die."

"Ah, yes," a finger flew into the air, and she stood up again. She stepped behind the chair and clutched its back, leaning on it, "but there is more to it than that."

"What more can there be to dying?"

"Our business is thousands of years old, as long as the breathers have died. We are the Told, and we set out to fulfil a need. The need isn't merely keeping the True Order of Life and Death. It is also to help those who are left behind."

If she was expecting a reaction, Cormac gave none. He was too busy trying to understand what she was saying. *Fulfil a need? Keep order? But what does any of it mean?*

Inade straightened, waved a hand in an arc behind her, and the wall at her back lit up with images. Images of people from all over the world, hugging, laughing, kissing, holding hands, smiling, enjoying life. The images, like footage projected onto the wall, whirled around and then finally settled into rectangles next to each other in a neat pattern. They kept playing, kept on being happy.

"This is our goal," Inade said, walking slowly towards the wall, arms outspread. "All of this: the happiness of the human race."

"Noble cause," Cormac said under his breath.

Inade whirled around and flew at him. She advanced on him so quickly, in a flash, she was leaning over him, a hand on his shoulder, her face very close to his. "You have no idea the struggles we have had, Cormac, the centuries of despair we've had to endure to try and keep the world spinning. Without happiness and love, where will they all be?" She looked at the wall but stayed as close as she was to him.

With another wave of her hand, the images of joy on the wall were replaced with scenes of war, dead bodies covered in flies, nuclear explosions, men killing other men, rage, hatred, despair. "It's happened before, more times than I'd like to count, that these things were all that was seen by the breathers. And each time, we have brought them back from the brink."

"The brink of what?" Cormac asked hesitantly, leaning away from her.

"Destruction."

It sounded ridiculous. *How could this group of whatever they are keep the world from destroying itself?* he thought.

"By making sure that people continue to love and hope, that's how."

How did she do that?

She answered his thoughts again. "Stop thinking so loudly, Cormac, and I won't."

"Can I do that?"

"Of course not," she answered briskly, pushing on him to lift herself up and striding away. She waved her hand again, and the images disappeared, the light around them returning to normal.

He decided to test this. *Can you hear all of my thoughts?* he questioned in his mind.

"Yes."

All the time?

"Yes, when I choose to listen."

"What about when I'm not here?"

"It's a little harder, but as soon as I find you, I can," she replied. "How do you think I found you just now?"

"You found me by listening for my thoughts?" He hadn't considered it before, how she had found him. He wondered how much of what had passed between him and Jiëlle she had heard. Or if she had intercepted Jiëlle's thoughts and not wanted her to take him wherever it was she had been leading him.

"Jiëlle was taking you to see Ludis, but we'll come back to that in a moment," she said, dismissing it with a wave of her hand. "For now, I want to show you something. Come here and give me your hands."

She stood next to her chair and held out her hands, palms face up. Slowly, he stood and shuffled towards her.

"Don't worry, I won't bite."

He could not help but chuckle at that. He held out his hands as she did. Suddenly, she grabbed his wrists tightly and inched towards him. She stared into his eyes, not blinking. Cormac tried to pull away, but she was holding onto him too tightly.

"What are you—"

"Don't fight me, Cormac," she interrupted. "Keep looking at me. Focus on me. Take in every aspect of my face, how tightly I'm holding you, the colour of my hair, the texture of my skin. Everything."

He tried, but it was difficult. She was holding onto him extremely tightly, almost cutting off the circulation to his hands. It was easy to focus on that, but it overwhelmed everything else she had said to concentration on. Her hair was dark brown, he could see that, and her eyes were grey, but seeing more specifics than that was difficult.

"Focus, Cormac," she ordered, squeezing his wrists tighter. "This is important."

"I'm trying."

"Stop trying, and do it."

Should I get used to this sort of cryptic talk from her? he wondered.

"Cormac ..." she drew his name out to show him that she could hear him and, more than likely, that she was little pleased with him.

"Sorry."

"Don't be sorry. Build a picture of me in your mind, exactly as you see me now."

"Why?"

"So that you can see me exactly as I am."

He closed his eyes and began to draw everything that he could see of Inade: her dark brown, wavy hair; her blue-grey eyes and the crow's feet around the edges; the tightness of her mouth; the way her black clothes hung from her shoulders to the ground; and this surprised him as he only then realised that they were at eye level, so she was quite tall.

"Good," Inade whispered, "good."

He could hear the smile in her voice, and the picture of her in his mind smiled too. The crow's feet bowed and emphasised her eyes; lines around her mouth that he had not noticed before curled around the upturned corners of her lips, revealing a slight dimple on her left cheek.

"Very good," she whispered again. She took a step back, still keeping hold of his wrists but not as tightly, and whispered, "Now open your eyes."

As Cormac did so, the white room was filled with flowing blue-green light. He looked around him and watched it flicker and dance across the walls. He looked back to Inade and saw that the light seemed to be shining from her, from inside her! The brightest part of the light poured from her centre. He smiled and looked around in awe.

"What is this?" he asked. It was so beautiful.

"It's my colour," she informed him.

Looking back at her, he asked, "What does that mean?"

Inade let go of Cormac and took a step back. "To switch it off, just blink your eyes and want it gone, and it will pass," she said. As she walked back to the chair, he noticed that the brightest part of the light followed her as she walked. It really was emanating from her innermost being.

Cormac did as she said, and when his eyes opened, everything was back to normal – white and oppressive. He sat down across from her again.

"In answer to your question," she began, crossing her legs and leaning back, "each person has a colour, an identifier which differentiates each person in the world. Like a fingerprint or DNA, if you will. We can use this fingerprint to find people when we are looking for them."

"Why would you need to find someone?" Cormac asked, confused.

"We are the Told, Cormac," Inade stressed, "the True Order of Life and Death. It is our duty, our reason for existing, to help the breathers, even when they cannot help themselves. When the breathers can't find their own people, *we* still need to be able to. We are there for them, to make transitioning easier, no matter who they are. Do you see?" She didn't wait for an answer. "The colours help us to find them when they can't be found by others so that, should something happen, we are there, and we are prepared. What we do requires us to always be able to find whomever we need to, whenever we need to. The challenge for a Guide is locating their charge; once that's done, the bonding takes over, and it's an easy job from there. Most of the time anyway. The colour is just one tool that we've developed over the many years we have been doing this to make it easier on everyone."

"And Joyce's dreams?" Cormac asked quickly, remembering what Joyce had told him. His mind was racing with more questions than he had had before. "Is that another tool that we have for – what did you call it – the bonding?"

"Your charge has had dreams about you?"

"She has."

Inade said nothing, staring off into the distance behind him. Cormac wondered if she had not heard of such a thing before. What would that mean about him? Was this a confirmation that he was different from everyone else, with his weird flashes and seeing the blurs so soon?

"It's not a usual way for the bonding to occur," Inade answered his unspoken questions. "But it seems to have worked well for you, so don't worry about it. It isn't unheard of, so no, it doesn't make you different."

"What are more usual ways?"

"Imprinting through touch or a word," she answered distantly, "that's more usual. It generates trust between the Guide and his or her charge so that the charge is more comfortable. Clearly, your charge needed some ... forewarning."

"And how did I find her?" Cormac asked. "It's not like I knew how to look for her colour. I just stepped into the elevator, and I was there, outside her house."

"I'm sure you've realised by now that Guides can travel through time and space," she said. "It's not as science fiction as it sounds. Our timelines are not linear like the breathers' are. This is necessary for us to do our jobs. Instead of waiting years and having multiple charges at once, we have the ability to focus on one, visit them as many times as we need to before they transition, and then move on to the next one. When you receive your charge, their colour is imparted to you so that, with only thinking about them, you can find them."

"So, me walking out of my room and into the restaurant where Joyce and her family were ... that's just how we move?" In a strange way, this was all making sense.

Inade scrutinised Cormac for a moment, frozen in her pose. Slowly, she sat up straighter. "You moved independently of the elevators?" she asked slowly, her voice low and still unnaturally oppressive to his ears.

With her question, the understanding he had found a moment before was replaced with worry. What if that wasn't how people – Guides – moved? There was something wrong with him. He was now certain of that.

Inade stood up and walked around the room again.

"That changes everything," she spoke almost to herself. "If he can move independently, that means that he isn't, for whatever reason, governed by the same laws as the rest of us—"

"What does that mean?" he interrupted. His heart was racing now. Surely they wouldn't allow him to carry on if he wasn't *governed by the same laws.*' They would need to fix him. And if they did that, would he still remember everything he knew now? Would he still remember Anele? Would she still remember him?

Inade froze. Slowly, she turned and faced Cormac, eyes narrowed. "Who is Anele?"

"Oh, um ..." he began, trying to think of anything but her. He couldn't let Inade see. He couldn't let her take Anele away from him, not when he knew so little about her. So, he thought about Joyce and where she was, and what she was doing. "No one." He hoped it would work, that changing his immediate thoughts could keep Inade out of his head.

"Hmmm," she breathed, clearly suspicious, but she didn't push the issue.

He wanted to change the subject, move it away from ... well, towards answers that he needed. Quickly, he asked, "What does it mean that I'm not governed by the same laws?"

Inade stood for a moment and looked closely at him. Then, she shrugged. "It means that you can move independently of the elevators." Her tone was dismissive. "I wouldn't worry about it, Cormac. It's just one thing that you can do that most others can't." She sat down again. There was clearly more that she wasn't telling him, but he wasn't going to push it. She linked her fingers together again and looked at Cormac. "Anything else?"

"You said you would tell me about why you stopped Jiëlle taking me to see ..." Cormac had forgotten the name in the moment.

"Ludis. Yes, I did," she agreed.

"Who is he?"

"Ludis is one of the Guardians," she explained, "one of the Told's leaders. He is in charge of Enforcement and would not have taken the story of your little episodes very well."

His heart sank. "So, you did hear that?" he sighed, still unaccustomed to how flat it sounded.

"Indeed," she straightened the fabric on her knee, "but that isn't anything to worry about either, Cormac. It happens."

That was a relief, and he felt his body relax from tension he had not known he was carrying. Though it didn't explain what he was seeing. He wasn't going to ask though. The thought of knowing what it was seemed too much to bear right now. He needed another change of topic. Focusing back on the colours, Cormac took a moment to formulate his question.

"So, how do I find someone's colour without being close to them?"

"You picture them in your mind," she said, as though the answer was a simple one. "Once you can see them, their colour becomes clearer, and you will then see where they are. Then, it's simply a question of getting to an elevator. Well, for most Guides, that's the way to do it. Or the other way."

"And I can find anyone?" he asked slowly.

"Why?"

"Say now I want to find Jiëlle, I can just close my eyes," he did so, "and picture her, and I will know where she is?" Almost instantly, he saw Jiëlle, red hair bobbing behind her as she walked very quickly. She looked very angry as she charged down a corridor. His eyes snapped open.

"Oh, yes," Inade's voice went up in delighted surprise, though it was still flat and unechoing. "Finding a Guide is easier than finding a breather, for sure."

"I see so," Cormac said, amazed that it had worked so quickly. "Does the colour always stay the same?"

"It does not, as a matter of fact," Inade was frowning at him now, but he could not tell why. "When a breather is marked for transition, which usually occurs between fifteen and twenty minutes before the event, their colour always changes to black, an almost light-sucking black. It gives off a hopeless feeling, like it's going to drain all the joy from the world. I'm sure it would, if it was given the chance."

This brought another question to his mind. "Is there any way of avoiding transitioning or delaying it?" Cormac worried that Inade might be troubled with where this line of questioning was going, but she answered nonetheless.

"No, there isn't," she answered simply. "To maintain the True Order, as we do, we cannot be responsible for deciding who transitions and who doesn't. To our true purpose, we must, well, remain true."

"Oh," was all Cormac could think to say. He thought about everything he had learnt in this strange room and then something Inade had said suddenly sunk in. "What did you mean, 'or the other way'?" he questioned hesitantly.

"There is a place I want to show you," she said. "It's between the breathers' realm and ours. We call it the Shade. It's a few seconds out of sync with reality and that is technically where we move through. Do you want to go see it?" she asked, a cheeky grin on her face.

Unable to think of anything else he wanted to ask, Cormac nodded his head and stood up. "Sure," he answered, "why not?"

Chapter

Four

THEY WERE STANDING on the corner of a busy intersection, shoulder to shoulder, watching the day go by.

There were cars whizzing along the streets and pedestrians walking about, everyone going about their business. It was very loud in comparison to the flat sound in the white room or even the hubbub in the foyer. Minibus taxis were hooting, people were talking, somewhere nearby someone was drilling and another hammering.

Looking around, Cormac noticed that those that passed them hardly seemed to notice them. Though the breathers made way to go around them, there wasn't so much as a glance at them. It was as though they weren't even there.

"This is a normal day here," Inade said. This was the first thing either of them had said since they had left the white room. Inade had not even answered his thoughts as they had walked towards the elevator.

Cormac decided to voice his observation, curious as to what the reason might be. "They don't seem to notice us."

Inade turned towards Cormac and nodded. "They only see what they want to see," she said. "Now, face me."

He turned towards her, pointedly looking straight at her.

"From the Shade, you will still be able to see all this," she began. "You will still be able to interact with everything around you. All the buttons that you can press, the cars you can touch, anything you'd like to interact with, you will still be able to when you concentrate on doing so. Otherwise, your presence will be unnoticeable to this world. Remember, we'll be a little bit out of sync, so things that look like they are there might not be any more or might not yet be there. Oh, and try to avoid walking through a breather, they tend to break into a shiver and get concerned.

"Finally," she urged, "keep in mind that all the Shade is, is a layer of existence over this one, one where *we* are *not* bound by the normal rules of movement, time, gravity, et cetera."

Cormac nodded his understanding. It was a lot to take in, but he suspected he would pick it up as they went along.

She looked at him, gave him a smile, and continued, using her hands to demonstrate. "Do exactly as I do. Lean on your left leg, push off the ground with your right foot, and spin to the left. Got that?"

He nodded again.

"Right foot swings, you spin to the left," she repeated, imitating the movement for Cormac to see.

Once again, a nod.

"Good. Then, the last thing is to block out the light from your eyes. Imagine it isn't there. Ready?"

He more than likely wasn't, but Inade didn't give him much of a choice.

"On the count of three. One, two …"

Cormac took a deep breath.

"Three!"

He watched Inade and did exactly as she did. His right foot pushed off the ground, while he was thinking about a place with no sunlight, and he spun around as hard as he could. He made a complete spin and ended up in the same place. Inade, on the other hand, was gone. Panic gripped him for a moment. What if he couldn't get there at all? He would have to try again and again until he succeeded. He couldn't give up. He wouldn't.

'That's the spirit, Cormac!' He heard Inade's voice in his head.

Heartened by her encouragement, he shook his limbs out and closed his eyes, imagining the entire area bathed in darkness, in a shade that was not nighttime but cold and normal all at the same time. He planted his left foot firmly in the red sand on the ground and rubbed it in to get an optimal grip. With his right foot, he pushed off the ground and spun around to the left. When he stopped, he planted his foot back down and only then opened his eyes.

It didn't work. He tried again and focused on all the details of what was around him: the brown trees with no leaves, the colour of the soil and the tar and the sidewalk, the noises of the cars and the taxis. Then, he closed his eyes and drew a picture of everything around him in his mind: the way the breeze was cold against his cheeks and blew through the trees, the smells from the restaurants across the road and from the people walking past him. Over this image in his mind, he drew a cloud that sent the area into shadow, cold and piercing. He lifted his right foot, and turning like he had suddenly realised he had walked the wrong way, he spun on the spot until he was facing the other way.

He felt a cold seep into his skin and a breeze that seemed to be blowing circles around him. He noticed that there wasn't much light now either; the glare of the sun through his eyelids had become less. And the smells had gone too. When he opened his eyes, Inade was standing in front of him, a smile on her face. He had done it!

His elation disappeared quickly when he felt the strangeness of the place crawl over him. Everything looked the same as it had before, the cars and people still shuffled by, but they moved slower and then faster. All the colours had turned into shades of grey. They also weren't fixed, they blurred in and out of focus, making some shapes bleed into others. He could even see the breeze he had felt blowing around him. Streams of different greys whirled around him, almost feeling at him to learn more about him.

"Welcome to the Shade, Cormac," Inade welcomed. Her voice was lower than normal, but whether it was put on for effect or because of where they were, Cormac couldn't tell. "From here, you can get to anywhere. We move like light here and can arrive anywhere we choose. It takes some practice though, so let's aim for ..." she looked around, then pointed, "down the street. See that STOP sign? We'll meet there."

Inade stared at the sign, leaned forwards as if to run, then vanished from the spot with a whirling blur left behind her. Cormac turned and looked at the STOP sign. It was four blocks away, and there stood Inade, leaning against the pole. She waved at him, her smugness palpable even at that distance.

Was she expecting him to fail again on his first try? He would show her. He had more or less figured out how Guides moved, so he was confident he could do it. He stared at the sign, pictured it in his mind, drawing in all the details, and flung himself towards it. It felt as though an invisible cord dragged him towards the sign by his navel so quickly that, when he got there, he nearly lost his footing. He grabbed hold of the pole, planted his feet on the ground, and straightened himself up.

"Not so difficult," Cormac boasted. He was quite proud of himself.

"Let's try again," she said. She seemed to be enjoying this as much as he was. She looked up at the tall building across the street. "Rooftop. Slightly tricky, but let's see what you make of it." She leaned into a run again and disappeared.

Cormac sighed and stared at the tall building. How was he supposed to get there if he didn't know what it looked like? He stared up at the building, taking in dark and light grey paint, the dirty windows and the five or six storeys it seemed to go up. He closed his eyes and brought up the image in his mind. Suddenly, he found himself moving up the building and seeing more of it, seeing the light paint bubble in some places and the staircases through the gaps of the darker grey slates. Then, he was looking down at the building. He could see Inade standing on the flat roof where the peeling light paint seemed to flake and drift into oblivion as he watched it. Her hands were on her hips, and she was looking down at him.

He had nothing to lose, so he leaned into it and let the invisible cord take him up to the top of the building. He only saw streaks of grey whiz past him, and in a second, he was next to Inade on the roof but lying face down.

"Well done," she said, smiling. "You're getting the hang of this."

She clapped a hand onto his collar and pulled him up.

"Thanks," he puffed. He was beginning to feel slightly tired after all the exertion.

"All right. let's try something more challenging now," Inade said. "Come find me."

She shot him a cheeky smile, her dimple showing again, and disappeared.

"But where d..." he trailed off. He was meant to find her, so obviously she wasn't going to tell him where she went.

He looked at his new surrounds. From his new vantage point, he could see the cars driving by in veins of grey, the people and activity below him carrying on as normal.

There was no sound but the sound of the wind blowing the greys around, and it made the Shade more unnerving. As he watched the world go by, he saw a group of what looked like university students standing against the palisade fence across the road.

Cormac closed his eyes and drew them in his mind. The invisible cord pulled him down to them, yet as he fell down on the ground, his legs went through one of the boy's legs. Cormac gawked at the boy as his knees went weak and he stumbled. The others laughed at him; not that he could hear anything except the wind, but he could see them laughing, mouths open, slapping each other on the backs, all in slow motion. Cormac stood up and frowned, wondering what more he could do.

He stood just behind the boy he had fallen through and whispered into his ear, "You have an itch on your elbow."

Astonishingly, the boy scratched his elbow while he continued talking, as though he didn't even know what he was doing.

Another test was necessary. Cormac blew gently on the boy's neck. The boy shivered and looked around. He would have looked right at Cormac if he wasn't in the Shade.

One last test. Cormac went to the boy standing next to the first and whispered into his ear, "You need to go home now."

A sudden look of realisation crossed the boy's face, and he waved to the others and began walking away.

Cormac was astounded. Clearly, he could affect the breathers more than what Inade had led him to believe.

Remembering he was supposed to find her, Cormac drew her water-colour blue-green colour into his mind: the way her hair fell around her face, the texture of her skin, the pinch between the eyebrows. Slowly, the image became clearer. He could see her, then where she was standing, and then all of her surroundings, the grey wisps lapping at the ends of her dress.

He leaned forwards and was quickly pulled along again, greys flying past him in a haze. A few seconds later, Cormac was flung into Inade. They went crashing to the floor. Inade pushed him off her and stood up, half pulling him up too.

"Good," she said, wincing slightly. "Just keep your feet out so you can stand when you land."

Cormac nodded. "Right," he acknowledged. "Thanks." He was panting now.

"Are you tired?" she asked.

"Just a bit out of breath," he replied, stretching his back.

"When was the last time you ate?"

"When I saw you in the common room, with all those others—other Guides."

"After this, let's get a meal." She looked a little concerned. "It will replenish your energy."

He nodded, agreeing that he needed that.

"For now, it's your turn," Inade said. "See where you can go, and I will find you."

Immediately, Cormac turned, picturing the pub he'd gone to with Anele, and dashed off. He was filled with renewed energy now and knew he could carry on a little longer. He felt much more in control this time, treating it like he was running, as opposed to being dragged, which worked much better.

The next thing he knew, he was there, in the room where he had sat with Anele and Hanna and the rest of them. The fire, grey and lifeless, slowly weaved this way and that in the fireplace, sending light-grey rays into the room. The lines on the brown couches, which now looked colourless, were swirling around in the winds in the Shade. He sat down on one and waited.

CHAPTER

FIVE

THE QUIET OF the Shade got really unnerving very quickly.

The only sound that he could hear was the winds of the Shade as they whirled around him, picking up his short hair and brushing his cheeks. Cormac distracted himself by watching the two groups of breathers that had been in the room when he got there. They moved in slow, jerking movements and laughed noiselessly. Cormac knew that it was because of the Shade that it looked so strange.

Time truly did pass strangely here, sometimes slowly and at other times too quickly. The Shade also made people sometimes look disfigured, gruesomely blurring their features in the wind. It was like he was back in the foyer, seeing those disturbingly hazy people again.

After what felt like an age of waiting, Cormac looked around him for a sign of colour: colour would have meant that Inade had found him. But there was none. Why hadn't she found him yet? It couldn't have been difficult; it had been so easy for him to find her.

Cormac decided to go locate her instead. He closed his eyes, pictured her colour, her face, and then found where she was. She was standing in a white room with worn red carpets, talking with a tall, bony man. He looked quite old, judging from the deep lines on his face, and it was a face that Cormac somehow knew. It was Ludis, the one that Jiëlle had been taking him to before Inade intercepted him, one of the leaders of the Told. Why was she talking to him? Why had she not come to find him?

Standing up, Cormac leaned into the wind and moved towards Inade. His heart gave one loud thump, and he was in the room with them. Something strange happened then: a pop sounded in his ears, like a pressure had been released, and he realised that he could hear them. The sounds of their voices seemed deafening compared to the silence from before.

"I'm telling you, Ludis, he doesn't have a colour," Inade urged.

"And I'm telling you, Azemik, that's *not* possible," Ludis admonished more forcefully.

"Be that as it may, it's still true."

"Did you really try to look for him? Or did you give up, like usual?"

"Don't start with me, Ludis. You know that's not how this works."

"You need to set it right again, Azemik. You still haven't made it up to me after the last time."

Their voices were drilling loudly into Cormac's head. He squeezed his hands over his ears and tried to block out the noise, but it was no good. His eyes squeezed tightly shut as their voices continued to scrape away at the inside of his head. He screamed noiselessly, trying to block them out, and fell to his knees. *Stop! Make it stop!* he cried. *How do I make it stop?*

Strong arms wrapped around him and pulled him out of the Shade. He collapsed to the floor, the arms were still around him.

"Relax, Cormac," Inade's voice caressed his ears now. "It's over."

Relaxing, Cormac opened his eyes slightly and was looking up at Inade's face, Ludis standing just behind her.

"Guides aren't meant to be in this realm *and* in the Shade," Ludis mused to himself.

But whether or not Cormac heard, it was difficult to say. The pressure in his head had squeezed him so tightly that all he could do was take a deep breath and faint.

CHAPTER

SIX

CORMAC AWOKE IN a bed. It wasn't his bed, nor was he in his room.

He was surrounded by light-coloured curtains on all sides, and there was a light above him. It was very bright. He tried to shield his eyes from it by lifting his hand, but he couldn't. Looking down, he saw that he was strapped down onto the bed. He pulled and heaved and wriggled and shook, but he soon realised that there were three or four straps, all the way down to his ankles.

"Hello?" he shouted. "Is anyone there?"

He didn't understand what was going on. The curtains near his feet flittered gently to one side. It must have been a breeze or something. Did that mean that someone had just walked in?

"Hello!" he cried again. "Hello? Is someone there?"

He railed against the restraints and kicked and squirmed and carried on calling. "This isn't funny! Just let me go!" There was a loud *'thwack'* by the foot of the bed, but no matter how much Cormac craned his neck, he couldn't see what had made the noise.

He froze when whispered voices travelled softly to him. He strained to hear what they were saying. Pinpointing the voices was easy; making out their words was much more difficult. Frustration gripped his body tightly.

"I can hear you!" he roared, still trying to break free from the restraints. "Don't think I can't. Now, let me go!"

The whispering stopped for a moment, then continued. He thought quickly, trying to gather himself so that he could find a way out. He looked around him for something, anything that might help tell him where he was or why. He didn't feel any different to how he did before. He didn't remember less, not that he could tell anyway: Joyce, Anele, Inade, all of them were still walking and talking in his memories. So why was he there?

He shut his eyes tightly and tried to see himself. He lifted himself up and looked down. He could see that he was lying on the bed with all of his clothes still on, even his boots, strapped down by thick, wide straps. Focusing harder, he saw the dirt that had fallen onto the bed from his boots and a clipboard that was lying face down on the floor near the foot of the bed. That must have been the thing he heard fall when he was kicking.

No, don't think about that, he commanded himself. Focus on who is in the room.

He drew farther back from himself, past the light, past the pale curtains, until he could see that there were eight or ten curtains drawn around beds in this room. They were all drawn closed, leaving a pathway down the centre of the room. There, between two curtains near the end of the room, stood two figures. They seemed to be arguing. The one's hands were flying about, pointing this way and that, then jabbing the other person's shoulder. The other knocked the first's hand away and pointed towards the last curtain, behind which Cormac was.

"I can see you!" he shouted. "Don't pretend like you can't hear me!"

The two people stopped. The second person nodded their head and walked out of the room. The curtains around him blew gently again and then hung still. The first approached him.

Cormac opened his eyes and began fighting again. The curtains were drawn apart with a brisk flick of the wrist and then quickly closed behind Inade.

"Let me out of this!" he demanded.

"Now, Cormac, just relax," she urged softly.

"How can I relax when you've got me like this?" he wailed as he writhed his whole body up and down. The bed creaked and groaned. "Let me go!"

"Soon," Inade cooed, "soon." She stood next to him and stroked his head. "Don't worry. Everything will be okay."

"It really won't be," he threatened.

The smile on Inade's face was serene. It made him feel even more unnerved. And the way she stroked his head made his stomach turn.

"What do you want from me?" he growled through clenched teeth.

The curtains flittered to the side again and heavy footfalls sounded beyond the curtain.

"Help!" Cormac called. "Help!"

"Now, now, don't be like that," she uttered gently.

As soon as the second person entered through the curtains, Inade took a step back.

"I've got it," he said. Cormac glared at him. His name was Hamnez, a Guide like him and Inade.

"*Good.*" Inade dragged the word out. "Now, let's give it to him."

They both began walking towards him, one on each side of the bed.

Cormac writhed and pulled away and resisted as much as he could.

"Hold him," Hamnez commanded.

"No!" Cormac cried. "No! Let me go! Help! Help! Someone help me!"

"Don't worry, Cormac," Inade uttered. "This won't hurt at all."

She grabbed his chin and forehead with her strong hands and pulled his mouth open. Cormac squirmed as much as he could to get out of her grip. Hamnez laid his forearm heavily onto Cormac's chest and pressed him down.

"Don't struggle," Inade whispered into his ear. "It'll all be over soon."

Hamnez pulled a small, thin vial out of his coat and pulled the cork out with his teeth.

Cormac thrashed as hard as he could to get free from them. He kicked his legs with more urgency, feeling the straps there becoming looser, needing to break free. He twisted his shoulders this way and that, but before he could throw them off, Hamnez had thrown the contents of the vial into his mouth.

Inade clamped his mouth shut and pinched his nose.

"Swallow, Cormac," she commanded forcefully.

The dark liquid tasted revolting: it felt like it bubbled and oozed its way into every corner of his mouth, coating everything with an acrid burn that would be forever charred and scorched. There was something worse though. He was running out of air. He had to breathe, had to gasp for air, but his mouth was being held closed, and his nose. He wriggled his body in tight, short movements, but he couldn't get loose. He thrashed again, hoping that would work, but it didn't. He could feel his lungs burn and claw at his throat for air, and he had only one option: swallow.

So, he did. The charcoal taste that coated his mouth singed everything as it went down. He could smell it burn everything as it went down through his closed nose. As soon as he swallowed, Inade and Hamnez took a step back. They watched him with intrigue, his glare seeming to have little effect on them. His mouth felt like it would never work again, but he pushed through the pain and spoke.

"What was that?" he rasped. Whatever that revolting stuff was, it had set a fire in his mouth, his throat, his lungs, that made it difficult for him to breathe. "What have you done?"

They said nothing but continued to watch him.

Suddenly, Cormac felt his heart race in his chest. Every inch of his skin began to burn. His fingers clenched into fists but then shot wide apart as the burning turned to needles all over his body. He screamed, loud and long, as the agony touched everything that was a part of his body.

And still, Inade and Hamnez stood and watched.

The last thing that Cormac saw before he blacked out was the two Guides leaning over him and whispering to one another.

CHAPTER

SEVEN

CORMAC AWOKE IN a bed. It was his bed, in his room.

He looked around him, feeling slightly groggy ... or was that the tiredness that had not yet left his body? The lamp that hung on the side of his locker was on. The warm light lit up the room, and by its soft glow, he could see that his boots were placed neatly on the ground next to the bed. He didn't remember putting them there, he realised as he turned to his side. He looked at them in confusion.

How had he gotten to his bed?

The last thing he remembered was ... was ... being in the Shade and waiting for Inade to find him. So, how had he gotten here? He must have given up, he decided after a moment, and come back. But why were his shoes positioned like that? He had never put them so neatly before. Well, all he had to go on was the previous time when he had kicked them off before getting into bed. So why would he have—

There was a knock on the door that intruded on his thoughts.

Cormac sat up and swung his long legs off the edge of the bed. "Come in," he said, rubbing his face. He more than likely had been so tired when he had returned that he didn't remember doing it, he concluded as the door swung open.

"Hello Cormac," Inade chimed with a smile.

"Hi Inade," he replied, looking up at her.

"How are you feeling?" she asked sweetly.

"A little bit tired, actually." He shook his head, as though it would shake the sleepiness from his mind.

"You didn't get a meal when we came back, did you?" she offered.

We? he wondered. *Did she find me? Did we return together?* He really couldn't remember.

"Of course we did," she giggled, once again answering questions he had not asked out loud.

He looked at her vacantly.

"Don't you remember?" She sat down next to him. "I found you in that restaurant, and then we returned here. I told you to go relax, get a meal, and then rest, while I went on with my business. Do you remember?"

He thought about it for a moment. As he pondered, it gradually all came back to him. That is what happened. He smiled at her, shook his head again, and gave a soft chuckle. "Yes," he said, "of course I remember. Sorry, I guess I'm still waking up."

Inade tapped him on the back a few times, smiling and nodding. "It's all right. I know you were tired when we returned."

She reached down and picked up his shoes. As she handed them to him, she added, "And you even put your shoes neatly. How lovely."

Cormac took the shoes from her with a small smile. "Yeah, I ... I must have." He put them down and began to pull them on.

She gave him another smile and stood up. As she walked towards the door, Cormac stopped what he was doing.

"Inade?" he asked.

"Yes?" she asked sweetly, stopping and turning back towards him.

"When you found me yesterday, Jiëlle was taking me to go speak to Ludis," he began. "Do you think I still should?"

"Oh, definitely not," she simpered. "If you have any questions, you can just ask me, okay?"

"Okay," he replied thoughtfully.

"Is that all?" she asked, in the same sweet tone.

"It's just that ..." he was trying to find the words.

"Just that what?" she asked, sitting beside him again and putting a comforting arm around his shoulders.

"It's just that I don't remember what I wanted to tell Ludis or ask him," he admitted, looking at her and frowning.

"Don't worry about that," she simpered again, hugging him with the arm that was around his shoulders. "It will come to you when you're not thinking about it." She gave him a smile, stood up, and walked to the door again. As she pulled it open, she stopped in the doorway and looked back at him. "Now, make sure you get a meal before going out again," she instructed. "We can't go more than a day without this realm's sustenance. Always remember that, okay?"

Cormac nodded. Perhaps that was the reason he felt exhausted, despite having just woken up.

Inade waved to him and closed the door.

He finished putting his shoes on and went to the common room. There were quite a few Guides there, including Akael and Caster who were sitting together at a table. They waved and smiled at Cormac as he passed them and then continued with their conversation.

Cormac picked up a mug from the long table and looked at the many taps on the wall. While he had enjoyed the golden syrup from the blue tap, he wanted to try something different. He looked at each, trying to pick one.

"I started from that side," a short man told Cormac, indicating listlessly to the far side with his hand, then swooped it along as he continued, "and went all the way to the other."

Cormac looked at the Guide at his elbow and smiled. His name was Norrym. He was a whole head and shoulders shorter than Cormac, with thinning dark hair. Norrym looked up at Cormac and nodded once.

"Now, I just go 'round and 'round," he indicated the motion with his hand, "so that I'm not stuck with deciding which tap to choose."

"Sounds like a good system," Cormac approved.

Norrym pointed to a black tap on the top row on the far right-hand side. "Just avoid that one," he suggested. "It's … unpleasant."

"I'll keep that in mind," Cormac replied with a nod.

Norrym suddenly grabbed Cormac's arm and pulled him down so that Cormac's ear was right by his mouth. He whispered hurriedly, "Don't let them take who you are, Cormac. Don't ever forget."

Jiëlle clapped a hand onto Norrym's shoulder, and he very quickly let go of Cormac's arm.

"What are you whispering about, Norry?" Jiëlle asked, a Cheshire grin on her pale face as she eyed both the men in turn.

An uneasy smile came to Norrym's face. "I was … I was … I was …" he stammered. He was clearly very nervous of her.

"He was telling me which taps are the best," Cormac jumped in.

"Yeah," Norrym breathed, "that's what I was doing."

"Oh, I see." Jiëlle laughed derisively. "Sharing your crazy with the new boy? How sweet."

"No, Jië," he stammered, "I wasn't, I swear."

"He was actually telling me that it's best to try them all," Cormac offered, "at least once." He wasn't sure what was going on between the two or why he felt he needed to protect Norrym, but he did. "Norrym also suggested that I try from the red tap over there first."

Cormac wasn't sure why he too lied to her, nonetheless, he kept his composure.

"Is that so, Norrym?" Jiëlle asked. She seemed taken aback by this.

Norrym looked up at Cormac, nervous and confused, but then quickly nodded his head. "Yes, that's exactly it," he asserted, then hurriedly added, "I was whispering it to him because the red one is my favourite."

"So, Jiëlle, you see," Cormac concluded, "there is nothing going on here more than a discussion on what meal to have. Not crazy at all."

"Hmmm ..." she snorted, glaring at them both. She began to walk towards the tables but added in a whisper to Norrym, "I'll be watching you."

Once she was gone, Norrym let out a breath. "Thanks, Cormac," he sighed, tapping Cormac on the arm. "She's been hounding me ever since ... well, for a long time."

Cormac was watching Jiëlle and only half listening. She picked up a mug, paused for the briefest of seconds, then went to the red tap. The liquid that came from it was a warm-red colour and thick.

"It isn't bad," Norrym added.

"Hmm?" Cormac asked, eyebrows raised as he turned back to the shorter man.

"I said that the red one isn't bad," he repeated. "It's fruity with a hint of ... I'm going to say wood. It's really the only way to describe it."

"Oh," Cormac answered in surprise. "That does sound good."

The two men waited for Jiëlle to get her meal and move away before Norrym got a mug of his own and a meal. Cormac went for the red tap while Norrym went for a cream tap with a flap for a handle. They walked together to a table, far away from the watchful red-head, and sat with their backs towards her. Before Cormac had even taken a sip, Norrym began.

"It wasn't my fault," he began, staring into the steaming mug. "I did everything by the book, but still, she got lost, and I got punished, and since then, Jiëlle has been on my case." Norrym grabbed Cormac's sleeve again and pulled him close. "It wasn't my fault, Cormac. How was I to know that the woman had an instability?"

Cormac nudged his head away from Norrym, looking at him in confusion. "Who, Jiëlle?"

"No, stupid," he snapped. "My charge."

Slowly, Cormac pried Norrym's hand from his sleeve and picked up his mug. Norrym seemed to scarcely notice; he was looking over his shoulder at Jiëlle, who was talking to three or four other Guides, chatting and laughing. While he had a chance, Cormac took a sip of the red liquid. Norrym was right about the fruit, which was the first thing that he tasted, and the rich waves of flavours came one after the other, even after he swallowed. The aftertaste that it left was much like what trees smell like, Cormac reasoned, and that was probably where Norrym got the 'hint of wood' comment. It was truly delicious, and it was making him feel better already.

Norrym looked back to Cormac and spoke in a low tone. "My charge didn't successfully transition, you see," he explained. "It wasn't *my* fault. It wasn't *her* fault. It was *hers*." He indicated Jiëlle with a nudge of his head and banged his fist on the table.

"How was it Jiëlle's fault?" Cormac asked and took another sip.

"When she got here, Jiëlle was the happy, cheery sort, the kind that would find a story to cheer you up. You know the type?"

Though he probably didn't know exactly what Norrym was talking about, Cormac's mind went straight to Anele, and he smiled. "Yes, I do," he admitted.

"But then something happened," Norrym continued, as conspiratorial as before. "For her, the Shapes took form the soonest out of anyone, and when that happened, she was taken to see Ludis. From then, she was never the same again."

Frowning, Cormac leaned forwards, finally understanding the need for a soft voice. "What do you mean?" he whispered.

"I mean, when she returned … about a week later," he whispered back, "Jiëlle had changed. You saw how scary she was just then. Is that the person you met before? She was your welcome party, wasn't she?"

Cormac confirmed this with a nod but was thinking about how she was when they met and how she was when he went to look for her … for … why had he gone to see her? Why couldn't he remember? But he did remember that she changed from angry at him to sweet very quickly. He had thought that that was because she wanted him to do something, but now he was thinking that it might have been something else.

"Why are you telling me all this?" Cormac asked, Norrym's story rattling around in his head.

"Because she was strong," Norrym said, sitting up straight. He flexed his arms as though he were going to show Cormac his muscles, "you know, strong, but also mentally and emotionally." He leaned closer to Cormac and murmured so softly Cormac almost didn't hear. "So, if they can get to her, they can get to you too."

"Why would *they* want to do that?" Cormac asked, matching his quietness.

"To make you do what they want you to do." Norrym looked over his shoulder, jumped a little, and then sat straight up again. "But don't worry," he suddenly exclaimed loudly, "if you have from the black tap, you won't die or anything." His eyes were darting to his shoulder the whole time he spoke.

Cormac glanced to where Norrym was looking and saw that Jiëlle was walking their way. He drained his mug and stood up, pushing his chair out with the backs of his knees. "Well, thanks for the advice on the taps." Cormac spoke loudly too. "It was very informative." Cormac pushed his chair in, tapped Norrym on the shoulder, and leaned in quickly. "But really, thank you," he whispered.

"Bye now," Cormac called more loudly as he walked towards the long table where the mugs sat. He placed his onto the table, and as he turned around, Jiëlle was right in front of him. She was grinning broadly.

"Hi Cormac," she said pleasantly.

"We saw each other not ten minutes ago," he indicated. He tried to step back, but he bumped into the table behind him.

"I'm sorry about Norrym," she said, ignoring his comment and still smiling. "He can be such a pest sometimes. I don't know why they don't just let him transition already; he's been here long enough."

"He seems all right to me," Cormac tried to step to the left, but Jiëlle stepped in front of him, and followed him again when he went right.

"You don't need to be nice to everyone, you know?" she offered. "Especially not to Norry-worry-wart."

Cormac grabbed the woman's small shoulders and moved her aside. "I thought we had left all that breather nonsense like childish name-calling and exclusion back in life," he opined. He did not wait for a response and quickly walked away. As he passed Norrym, who had been watching the interaction, Cormac concealed a thumbs-up to the man, then left the room.

There was a little crazier and more random happening this morning than Cormac felt comfortable with. At least he knew one thing for sure, Jiëlle could not be trusted, and Inade and Norrym could be. They had both proven that since he had awoken.

As he walked down the corridors, Cormac realised that he felt much better than when he had woken up. He was feeling stronger, more confident, more alive than he had in a long time. The next question was what he should do next. He thought that he would sit in his quiet room for a moment and think about things, so he headed that way.

As he turned a corner, his mind wandered to his charge. He wondered how Joyce would be doing. When he visited again, it would be her dying day. That was not something he was looking forward to. How would those who cared for her react? Hanna? The other sisters? They all seemed to care for Joyce very much. And what about Anele?

He rounded another corner. She would be the best person to comfort Hanna, Cormac thought. They were best friends, after all, and when one loses a loved one, who better to comfort you? And Anele seemed amazing, he found himself admiring, and a picture of her came into his mind. How beautiful her hair was, the way her dark eyes drew him into a happy place, and her voice made everything better.

Cormac took hold of the handle of his bedroom's door, smiling to himself, and pushed it open, but his smile quickly faded when he saw where he was.

ROBYN ANAKIN VEARY

Part Three:

Tangle

CHAPTER

HE WAS STANDING in a short entrance hall, only a few metres long but just as wide. To his left was a doorway, which seemed to lead into a kitchen, and straight ahead, where the entrance hall ended, it opened onto a large living area. Cormac realised he was holding onto the doorknob so tightly it made his hand ache. Once again, he had appeared somewhere without using the elevator and without knowing how, and this made him nervous.

A voice called from around the corner. "Han, is that you?"

It was a soft and kind voice, the voice he had been thinking of a moment before he arrived, one that soothed his nerves.

"Anele?" he called, hoping beyond hope it was her.

"Who's that?" the voice cried, as papers crashed to the floor. Cormac heard the voice curse, and then there was a scurry of movement. Anele came trotting around the corner, seemingly preoccupied, and when she saw him, she stopped. Her eyes sparkled with light and a half smile.

"Cormac?" she sounded. "Wha..." she breathed. She took a deep breath, shook her head, and took a step closer. "What are you doing here? How did you get in?"

Cormac looked at the latches on the door. He assumed that they had been locked before he did the impossible and travelled without using the elevators. "I ... uh," he began, looking back at her, "I just opened the door when there was no answer."

She walked to the door, took it from him, and closed it. She looked at it for a second, opened it, then closed it again. "I must have forgotten to lock it again." It didn't seem like she was talking to him. "Han is going to kill me!"

"I hope it's okay that I came over," he offered as a distraction from the door. If she knew the real answer to her question ... well, he wasn't sure he would be able to explain that.

Anele shrugged her shoulders at the door, looked up at Cormac, and smiled. "Of course it is," she answered and walked into the kitchen. "Would you like some tea or coffee?"

He wasn't sure about a breather beverage right now, but when he saw that she took two mugs from the basin, he nodded his head. "I'll have what you're having, thanks," was the best answer he could come up with.

In all honesty, he couldn't say why he was there. He had, after all, appeared, it seemed, because he thought about her. Cormac was beginning to suspect that that was how it worked. He had thought about Joyce before and walked out into the restaurant where she was; it seemed to him that the same thing happened here. Thinking about the person must be the key—the literal key to walk into the room where they are. This realisation made him chuckle softly.

As Anele pottered around the long kitchen and made them coffee, she talked in a very casual way, as though this sort of thing happened often.

"It's been so long since I've seen you," she began. "That night at Papa Joe's? That was a few months ago, two, two and a half, maybe. Strange, I don't remember telling you where I live. But you look good, a little pale maybe, but good. Have you been well? I honestly can't remember when it was that I saw you. I mean, I remember that night but what day was it? Was it a Saturday?" She stopped suddenly, leaned on the counter, teaspoon dangling half out of her hand, and put the other hand on her hip.

"I think it was a Friday," Cormac offered, though he honestly had no clue.

"You're right!" she answered triumphantly, brandishing the teaspoon at him. "It was a Friday! 'Cause Han, Erica, Aleiah, and I still went to that market thingy the next day, and that only happens on Saturdays. There we go, mystery solved!"

Cormac looked at the beautiful woman. She was wearing dark blue jeans, a baggy hoodie that had a picture of an owl on it, and her hair was tied up behind her head. She didn't have shoes on but was wearing stripy socks. She seemed so comfortable and so at home in her own skin.

Anele smiled and passed Cormac a steaming mug. "I'm sorry I'm so all over the place," she continued as she walked towards the lounge. "I'm busy studying for my last exam, and I'm a little behind schedule. I was supposed to be finished with Hydraulics already, but …"

It very quickly became apparent why Anele felt she was both mentally and physically all over the place. In the lounge, there were two couches that faced a large TV cabinet, and between the couches and cabinet, there was a carpet that was covered with papers, books, stationery, a calculator, a ruler, and a few coffee-stained mugs.

"I see," was all Cormac could think to say. She made him quite nervous, he realised with a small smile. The churning of his stomach made it difficult to swallow, yet he felt the constant need to swallow, for reasons he could not explain. But all the same, he liked the feeling.

"You disappeared that night!" Anele accused, jabbing a finger into his chest. "Where'd you go? Andrew swore that you literally disappeared, but he'd had so much wine at Granny Joyce's birthday that I hardly believed a word. But you," she jabbed him again, "you did disappear. No goodbye. No sorry. No 'I don't actually want to spend time with you, so I'm outta here'. Nothin'!"

Cormac stared down at the gorgeous woman. Her voice sounded angry, but her face said something else. She wore a cheeky smile and a devilish sparkle danced in her eyes. That told Cormac she wasn't being too serious but that there was an element of truth in what she was saying.

Unsure as to how to react, Cormac sighed. "I'm so sorry," he murmured. "I should have said something. I was feeling so sick that I was worried that speaking might end badly." He realised that he wasn't sure at all why he had felt sick or why he had left. All he remembered was a desperate need to leave.

Anele laughed. It was a warm laugh, one from the pit of her belly, and it was joyful and honest. Cormac couldn't help but laugh a little too. He was happy that she didn't hold it against him. Looking back towards the papers on the floor, Cormac frowned.

"I hope I'm not interrupting?" Cormac asked.

"No," Anele assured, "I lost focus on this stupid subject about half an hour ago anyway, so a break is not the worst idea."

She gestured towards the couch. Scooping up a pile of papers, Cormac moved it to the seat next to it and carefully sat down. She copied his motion, moving the pile up yet again, then settled next to him and pulled one leg up, tucking her foot under the other leg. She rested her elbow on the back of the couch and looked at Cormac.

Sitting rigidly upright, Cormac wasn't sure what to do. She was smiling at him and staring. It made him feel slightly uncomfortable, but he couldn't help smiling too.

"Okay," she said at last. "Tell me, why are you here, Cormac? Don't see you in months, don't give you my number or any way of finding me, yet you do. Tell me, and be honest … are you a magician?"

Could he explain to her what he was? No, more than likely not. It wasn't ever explicitly said to him that he couldn't share what he was with breathers, but logically, it made sense not to. So, what could he say? And why was he actually there? Was it only because he had thought about her while he happened to be walking through a door? Or was it his attempt to make contact again, to see her once more? Slowly, he realised that all he wanted was to spend time with her and get to know her. But could he share that with her?

"I looked you up," he replied. "I went out of town for a while, and I got back this morning. I wanted to apologise for leaving the way I did."

"Oh, that's all right," Anele said with a dismissive wave of her hand.

"I really am sorry," he emphasised. "I wanted to stay, but I really wasn't feeling good."

Months had passed for her, then again, it had only been a short while for him. It was weird to think that their timelines connected so strangely. He wondered for half a moment if he had any control over when he would see her if he returned to where the Guides operated from.

Anele stood up and sat in the middle of her papers. She began to sort them out. "Please don't worry about it." She smiled as she made herself comfortable.

"What are you doing?" he asked, leaning forwards.

"Hanna will be home soon, and we're going to go get some groceries," she said as she picked up this page, put it with others, closed that book, placed it next to her, "so I want to have this all cleared away before she gets here. She doesn't like mess." It almost sounded like she wanted to laugh but intense concentration took over.

"Okay," he uttered, "Should I leave?" He began to stand up.

"No, no," she hurriedly replied, reaching out a hand to him. "Please don't. I'd like for you to stay. At least stay for dinner."

He froze at her response, then slowly smiled. "All right," he replied. He stretched his hand towards hers and took hold of it. She squeezed his, gave him a pleased smile, and then continued with sorting out her papers.

In the meantime, Cormac stood up and looked at the TV cabinet. It was large, almost filling the whole wall. It had one large window, where the TV sat, with many smaller windows haphazardly arranged around it. In some of the windows, there were books, in others, there were photo frames. He looked at the photos and smiled at the happy times that they showed.

One caught his eye. Cormac reached up and took the photo down. In it, there was a group of people, smiling and hanging on one another. He recognised Anele in the middle with a man behind her, who had his arms around her shoulders. It felt familiar to him somehow, like he had seen this before … no, it was more than that.

"When was this taken?" Cormac asked, holding out the picture for her to look at.

Anele leaned forwards and looked at the picture. "It'll be a year ago on the eighth of July," she said. "It was a friend of ours' birthday. His birthday," she pointed at the man hugging her.

A year ago. How strange. It couldn't have been him. He couldn't have been there, but it looked so familiar, so much like he knew the people and he knew something … something that made him think that, somehow, he and

Anele were connected before they met for the first time at Joyce's birthday.

"Where did you go to celebrate?" he asked quietly.

"His favourite place, of course," she chuckled and rolled her eyes. "It's called Delta Tor, out towards Centurion." A sad look came over her face though. "Maybe if we hadn't gone there ..."

Cormac looked at her, puzzled by her tone. She seemed sad. "What happened?" he whispered.

Anele's shoulders dropped as she looked down. "He ..." she hesitated. "He ... died."

"I'm sorry." He spoke in the same soft tone. He knelt next to her and put a hand on her shoulder, unsure of anything else that he could do.

Quickly, she rolled onto her knees and hugged him, burying her face in his shoulder. Surprised for a second, Cormac almost lost his balance, but as she began to cry, he put his arms around her and held her tightly.

CHAPTER

THEY SAT ON the couch for a while, talking about JP, who died in a car accident on his birthday. Anele's hands were linked around Cormac's.

"He was my best friend," she continued, with a sniff. "I still can't believe he's gone. He was the best person I knew."

A tear rolled down her cheek again. Cormac reached up and wiped it away gently.

They sat there for a time. Anele did most of the talking, and he just listened. He was glad to be the one who was there for her. It didn't seem like she had talked about JP or what had happened to him since it happened. She shared a story with him about when their group of friends had gone to a place called *Magnolia Dell* and played, like children, on the slides and swings. They had had a great day and, Anele admitted, that that was the first time that she realised she had feelings for JP. She didn't want to say anything until she was certain, but she never got the chance. The night of his birthday party, where that photo had been taken, they had gotten separated and never got that moment alone that she had been hoping for.

Once she was finished with her story, she hugged Cormac again and thanked him for listening to her whine and that she was feeling strong enough to continue with packing up. Cormac replaced the picture, still eerily sure he had some connection with it.

Once everything was cleared away, Anele stood in the middle of the now tidy lounge, hands on her hips, and looked around. She smiled with pride, but it faded when a look of realisation crossed her face.

"What's the time?" she said to herself. She looked up at the clock on the wall. "Han should be here any minute now," she told Cormac. "Then we'll hit the shops and get cooking."

Hanna arrived, as Anele predicted, a few minutes later, and the three drove to a large shop with the words 'BEST AND FRESH' on a big sign above the large entrance way. Hanna, who had seemed only a little surprised to see Cormac, explained as they walked in that Anele's parents owned the store and that they gave them family discount on whatever they wanted.

They first went to the office where a short, round brunette woman sat behind a desk. She jumped up the moment she saw Anele and cried, "*My liefste!*" as she grabbed and hugged her.

Hanna and Cormac stood in the doorway as they hugged. Hanna leaned towards Cormac and whispered, "She's a very sweet woman," she explained, "and *very* excitable."

Cormac nodded and smiled. He could certainly see that.

"*Hallo Moeder,*" Anele squeaked and gave the woman a kiss. "Where's *Baba*?"

"You know him," the small woman replied with a smile. "Always on the floor and working with his men."

Anele and the woman laughed, the exact same sound coming from both of them. This made Cormac smile, warmed by their connection. Then, Hanna stepped forwards and gave the woman a hug. They exchanged pleasantries and more laughter, and it made the warmth spread all over him. The warmth quickly froze when he suddenly felt Anele pull him forwards.

"*Moeder*, this is Cormac," Anele introduced. "Cormac, this is my mother, Riette."

They shook hands. "Hello," Cormac said stiffly.

"*Hy's mooi*," Riette told her daughter.

Anele gasped and slapped her mother on the arm, then giggled. She shot her mother a wink. "Can we just help ourselves?" she asked.

"You ask every time, and every time is the same answer," Riette answered, suddenly serious. "Of course you can. Remember though to bring it to me before you leave so I can write it up."

They nodded, agreed, and left.

Hanna grabbed a trolley and pulled out her shopping list. They walked around the store, picking up whatever Hanna told them to: fruit, vegetables, bread, meat, this, that, the other. It wasn't very exciting, but Cormac enjoyed seeing how Anele and Hanna interacted. They laughed a lot, made jokes about rude looking fruit – which Cormac didn't understand – and then they very easily switched over to serious things, like how their exams were going and what they thought would happen in the following year's elections.

Anele left their grocery search to go find her father and pulled Cormac with her. Anele introduced her father as Thokozile. He was a tall, dark-skinned man, with a slender build and a large smile that matched his wife's. Anele and Thokozile began to talk. Hanna made a bee-line towards Cormac and, grabbing him by the elbow of his jacket, dragged him away.

"Don't worry about them," Hanna reassured him. "They do this every time. She'll say something, he'll poke fun, she'll take it too seriously, he'll poke fun, she'll poke fun, and the next thing you know, fifteen minutes have gone by, and the shopping still isn't done."

"They own this place?" Cormac asked, amazed at the scale of it all. They sold everything he could have thought of buying and more. Hanna explained that when they met, Anele's parents loved to grow their own fresh produce, so they decided to cultivate that into a business. It had developed into a nationwide chain of stores, each with its own locally grown farm produce, as far as possible.

In no time at all, they had everything on Hanna's list (and a bit extra), and they went to go see Riette again. The short woman hugged them again and thanked them for bringing Anele. She then also insisted that they must bring Cormac around for dinner soon. Hanna laughed but quickly tried to cover it up with a cough.

"We'll try, *tannie*," Hanna answered for him, "soon."

Satisfied with that answer, Riette waved them off. Anele joined them by the car in the parking lot not too long after and helped unpack the trolley.

Chapter

Three

Once they had gotten back to Anele and Hanna's flat and unpacked all the groceries, the two women started cooking. While they cooked, Hanna opened a bottle of wine, and they all enjoyed a few glasses. Anele put some music on while they were busy and soon the two were dancing in the kitchen, while Cormac sat on a stool. They had chastised him for being in the way and then relegated him to a chair that they put in the entrance to the kitchen. After knocking a third thing off the counter as he went to sit down, Cormac decided that it was the best place for him.

They ate and laughed and talked about their lives, and the whole time, Cormac had that same bizarre feeling that this was familiar. He was comfortable and really enjoyed himself, but throughout the evening, it played in the back of his mind. Had he been here before? Had he done this before, shared a meal with the two of them and enjoyed their company so much?

After dinner, Hanna suggested that they watch a movie. There was some debate over which movie to watch, but eventually, they decided on an action. The two both agreed that watching the lead actor without his shirt on for most of the movie was one of its biggest attractions. The other attractions were all the explosions and the bad puns that were thrown around. It made them laugh and their laughter made Cormac laugh.

Is this what it's like to be a breather? he found himself pondering.

No wonder the breathers didn't like the idea of transitioning.

When the movie was finished, Hanna said good night and went to bed. Not wanting to keep Anele from doing the same, Cormac decided that he should go. Anele walked him to the door where they stood in silence.

At last, Anele spoke, "Thanks for tracking me down."

"It was my pleasure," he answered sincerely.

"By the way," she said, "did you have that checked out? Your fit, I mean."

"My fit?" Cormac repeated, confused.

"That episode that you had when we were at Papa Joe's?" she pushed gently. "Which left you on your back and unconscious for a few heartbeats too long? You remember?"

He didn't. He definitely had no memory about a seizure of any sort. He remembered being there, then feeling terrible and sitting in the bathroom. How could he not remember that? How could he have lost that chunk of his memory? Surely something like a seizure would stick out in his memory. Surely? But he couldn't tell her that he didn't remember. It made his heart ache to think that there was so much that he couldn't tell her.

"Oh, yeah," he answered, "it turns out it was nothing."

"Seemed like a pretty serious something to me," Anele opined, "but hey, I'm no doctor."

Cormac chuckled, but he was distracted by his worry. *Is it normal for a Guide to lose memories?*

"Well, good night," she said and stepped forwards for a hug.

He hugged her back and noticed that she held on a little longer than usual.

"Good night," he said.

"Will I see you soon?" she asked.

"When is your last exam?"

"Tuesday, so five days away," she seemed excited to get this last exam out of the way.

"I'll see you on Tuesday then."

With that, Cormac turned and left. He ran this new information around in his head as he walked down the walkway, the clear night sky above him blowing cold and doubt at him. Perhaps a good night's sleep might do him some good, even though, when he thought about it, he hadn't been awake for very long.

As he walked down the walkway, he glanced over the railing to his right, then towards the door and the EXIT sign at the end. When he got there, he pulled the door open, thinking about resting, and found himself in his little room. He looked behind him and saw that it wasn't the passageway he had just walked down but the corridor that led past his and the other rooms.

Too exhausted to think about it now, Cormac closed his door, kicked off his shoes, and fell into a deep sleep.

CHAPTER

FOUR

AS TIME WENT by, Cormac got better at being on time. The first time he returned to visit Anele, he was off by a week. His excuse was that he thought that she had meant the Tuesday after next. She laughed and didn't ask about it again. For the next visit, he was three days late, and from then on only ever as much as a few hours. Clearly, it took practice, and practice he did. He was happy to do it, as it meant spending time with Anele. She made him laugh, and somehow, he made her laugh too.

Cormac spent most of his waking time with her. The rest of the time, he would return to HQ, as he was now calling it, for sleep and sustenance. He got into the routine of returning to his room, resting, then going to get a meal in the common room, before going to visit Anele.

While in the common room, Cormac rarely saw Jiëlle, but Norrym was there every time. The first time, Norrym took a meal from a grey ornate tap and joined Cormac on the couches.

"Have you lost anything?" Norrym asked cryptically.

Cormac looked at the balding man and wondered just how much he knew and how he knew it.

"I have, as a matter of fact," Cormac answered. "I seem to have lost some memories."

Norrym seemed harmless enough, however, Cormac's certainty about trusting him was waning. If he knew what was happening to Cormac, why wouldn't he say? And if he didn't know as much as he hinted that he did, why was he pretending?

"That's how it starts," Norrym sighed. He took a sip of his thick, light-yellow meal. He looked around the room before leaning close to Cormac. "They take a few small memories, and then they take the important ones, and then they start removing all of them so that you don't remember anything about a person or a place."

"Why?" Cormac asked hurriedly.

"Why what?" Norrym asked indignantly. "Why do they take memories?" He barked a laugh. "To control you!"

Cormac leaned close like Norrym had done. "Don't they already control us?" he whispered.

Norrym looked stunned by this question. He didn't say anything more, so Cormac finished his meal and left.

Their conversations always revolved around Cormac losing something important. Cormac knew straight away that Norrym was onto something, but no matter how hard he tried, Cormac couldn't remember the things he realised he couldn't. Norrym kept suggesting tricks that he should try: meditating, recreating the events that he did remember, even lying on his bed with his legs in the air and his head dangling over the edge.

When Cormac eventually tried that, there was a shudder that ran through him. Something did spark a memory, or the hint of one, but he wasn't sure. So, he sat up on his bed, then rolled onto his back and hung his head again. There it was, the flash, no, a sinking feeling that his brain was going to slip out of his head. He knew that feeling. Somehow, he'd had it before. But when? He tried it a few more times, and each time, the spark grew brighter and brighter until, finally, it burst into a bright flame. He was remembering falling down, but there was something more … something he saw when he was like this … something … transparent?

Frustrated that he couldn't figure it out, he gave it up as a bad job and decided to go visit Anele.

Norrym also warned Cormac that their movements were tracked within HQ. As a result, Cormac only moved between the common room and his room. It made things easier for him as his door was perfect for getting to Anele. In addition, there was nowhere else he wanted to be besides with Anele, and when he was in HQ, the common room and his room were the only places he needed to be in.

He noted the passage of time carefully. For Cormac, it had been no time at all; yet for Anele, three months went by.

He was loving spending so much time with her. They did everything together, and it was usually Anele who surprised him with exciting suggestions of things to do. So when, one afternoon, she suggested they go for a drive, he didn't question but happily agreed. Where they were going, Anele would not say. Cormac didn't mind though as he loved the surprises that she thought up for him. They were usually amazing. One afternoon, they went for a picnic in a park and watched people walking around them for a few hours. Another time, she took him to see a movie in a movie theatre. That was a great experience. And just like with all of those times, on this day, she had that same playful glint in her eyes.

She was also trying to get him more confident about driving. He clearly knew how to, some sort of weird muscle memory that stayed with him through his transition. She gave him directions as he drove, and they talked about things, like they always did.

After a comfortable silence of a few minutes, Anele asked, "Why are you with me?"

"What do you mean?" he asked, giving her a quick glance. He wasn't that comfortable about not watching the road while he drove.

"I mean," she began and sighed, "I like you, a lot actually, and I love spending all this time with you, but ..."

"But ..." he tried. "But why am I spending all *my* time with *you*?"

"Yes!" She seemed relieved and comforted that he had found the words that she could not.

"For the same reason you spend your time with me," he answered simply. "Because I like you a lot too."

This answer made Anele grin from ear to ear. "Really?" she squeaked with glee.

"Really."

"That's awesome," she said, visibly relaxing.

"Why would you even need to ask?" he enquired, suddenly worried that she didn't know how much she meant to him. While he knew that he had never explicitly said it, he had hoped that she had realised it from his actions.

"Because it means that this trip is going to be a good one," she answered.

"How so?" he asked.

"Turn left up here," she said.

He did so and asked his question again, but she didn't answer.

"It's this house here, this one on the right," was all she said, indicating the short driveway with her hand.

They pulled up in the driveway of a small, old-fashioned house. The garden in front was small, with a low wall along a wide sidewalk. As they got out of the car, the front door opened and out walked two older people, their arms around one another. As they walked towards the car, and he saw them more clearly, Cormac realised where they were: at Anele's parents' house.

"Anele ..." He sighed.

"Don't worry, it'll be great!" she replied and got out of the car.

"*My liefste!*" shrieked Riette, who flung her arms up and waddled towards her daughter. She looked even shorter and even paler next to her tall, dark husband, and it brought a smile to Cormac's face. She pulled Anele into a tight embrace.

"*Hallo, my moeder!*" Anele breathed and hugged the woman back.

Cormac walked up, trying to maintain an even smile, as Anele was hugging her father. He knew how important her parents were to her and how important this gathering would be. He would have to be on his best behaviour, he told himself, trying to breathe normally. It suddenly felt like there was a lot of pressure on him to impress her parents and be accepted by them. Most importantly, he would have to remain calm and not freak out, nor run away by walking through a door and disappearing. He knew he couldn't do that. So, he smiled as best he could and took long, deep breaths.

"*Moeder, Baba,*" Anele said, stepping aside with one arm still around her father, "you remember Cormac?"

Both parents smiled and confirmed that they did by, in turn, hugging him tightly and welcoming him to their home. This helped Cormac breathe more easily.

Their house was not at all as it seemed from the outside. It was spacious, and there were many pieces of furniture in each room that they walked through. They went through the house and into the kitchen.

"Just in time," Thokozile chortled as he handed Cormac two bowls with a transparent cover over them. "We were about to start worrying that you'd miss lunch completely."

Riette and Anele laughed at this as they picked up dishes and went outside to the back garden. On the grass was a white plastic table, with more food on it. They juggled some dishes around and managed to fit everything on. It was only when Riette remembered drinks and shuffled inside that Cormac noticed an old man at the end of the table. It was hard not to, the way the old man shouted after her.

"Gin and *Dry Lemon*, Etty," he called after her.

Anele grabbed Cormac's hand and held it tightly. She led him towards the old man and said, "Hello Geegee," Anele gave him a hug and he patted her on the back with one hand. She took Cormac's hand again and added, "Geegee, this is Cormac. Cormac, this is my grandfather."

Geegee tried to stand, but he didn't make it very far. Cormac plunged forwards and offered his hand.

"It's lovely to meet you," Cormac said. As they shook hands, he gave Anele a smile. She smiled back at him. It amazed him that her smile still made him feel like his heart would float away from all the happiness inside of it.

Riette called for help from inside. Thoko, as he insisted on being called, ran in to help her. When they returned, Thoko was carrying a tray with clinking glasses, Riette at his elbow. She handed out the drinks, kissed her husband on the cheek, and then everyone sat down for their meal. They ate and talked the afternoon away. Riette was an excellent cook as it turned out, although it was revealed that Thoko had made the desserts. They talked about all sorts of things: Anele's studies, Cormac's fake studies, the friends they had, her parents' business, which seemed to be doing extremely well, and Geegee's new girlfriend. Her name was Lily, and she was apparently the most beautiful woman at the bowls club where Geegee spent his afternoons twice a week.

All too soon, the sun had set, and the stars were starting to peek out. The warm night air was fresh, and a sweet smell floated their way. Riette very proudly boasted about Thoko's night flowering plants. They smelt amazing.

Geegee, who seemed little concerned with the conversation that went on around him, called Cormac over and started discussing the stars, pointing out all his favourite constellations.

"The best stars in all the world, right here, in our garden," Riette said, taking Thoko's hand and smiling.

"Ah, definitely," Thoko agreed, smiling back at her. "And the most beautiful women, right, Cormac?"

Cormac wasn't sure how to answer that. He looked down and felt his face turn hot.

"*Baba!*" Anele chastised.

"Your mother is the most beautiful woman in all the world," Thoko said and kissed his wife's hand. Riette smiled up at him as he continued, "and you know you are my *most* beautiful daughter, Anele, and you cannot argue."

"I'm your only daughter, *Baba!*"

Cormac laughed at this, and so did Riette and Thokozile. It was wonderful to be with her and her parents on such a lovely evening.

Around dinner time, more food was prepared, and they all helped. Cormac mainly waited to be ordered around as it turned out that he wasn't very good in a kitchen, Anele frequently commented. He noted that they seemed to work so well together as a family; watching them made him smile a lot. They also seemed to like making jokes and making each other laugh, and they all had the same endless amounts of energy for everything. It was very clear that they were close.

After dinner, they sat under the stars, drinking coffee and talking. Cormac was getting used to the bitter drink. Thoko made a joke about his wife and coffee, and Riette scrunched her nose up at him.

"I only started drinking coffee because of you, Anele," Cormac playfully chided, with a small smile, and he poked her gently in the side.

Anele smacked his hand away and laughed. "There's a lot of things that I've introduced you to," she jabbed back.

Riette laughed. She laughed a lot, a light, infectious laugh that was often caught by everyone. Thoko began to tell a story about making Riette laugh when she first met his parents, and she somehow snorted coffee out of her nose. By the end of the story, almost everyone was guffawing hard, with tears welling up in Riette's eyes. Cormac looked over at Geegee, clutching his side against the laughter pangs, and noticed that he was again not joining in. Instead, Geegee was sitting quietly and staring up at the sky.

"What are you seeing, Geegee?" Cormac asked while the others continued talking.

The old man didn't look at Cormac when he answered. "The stars are looking fantastic tonight, Cormac."

Cormac looked up and saw more stars than before and that they twinkled brightly. It was, as Geegee said, fantastic. He had wondered why Geegee was so fascinated with the stars, but as he looked up at them, he began to understand.

Riette leaned over towards Anele. "He's been doing this every evening this week," she whispered. "He keeps talking about how they dance. It makes no sense."

"They do, Etty," Geegee scolded, looking at her angrily. "Just because your young eyes can't see it, doesn't mean it's not happening." And with that, he looked up again.

Riette and Thoko exchanged a look.

Anele coughed and began to stand up. "Well, I think we should be off. Don't want to get home too late."

Cormac quickly stood up to pull out her chair.

"Thanks," she whispered to him.

He smiled at her and then looked at her parents. "Thank you for everything," Cormac said.

Riette and Thoko were on their feet now too.

"Must you go?" Riette asked sadly.

"The spare rooms are ready for you," Thoko added.

Anele shook her head. "No, thanks, *Baba*," she answered. "We can have a sleepover next time."

Slowly, they made their way towards the house, still talking and laughing.

"There! Quickly! Look!" Geegee called after them, jumping to his feet and pointing straight above him.

They all looked up.

"What is it, Geegee?" Thokozile asked.

"There it is again!" he shrieked, giddy as a schoolgirl.

"What is it, Papa?" Riette asked impatiently, searching but not seeing what he was pointing at.

"The stream of shooting stars dancing across the sky," Geegee said, swaying from side to side. "Don't tell me you can't see that, girl?"

"I'm sorry, Papa," Riette sighed, "I can't see them. Can any of you?"

Everyone shook their heads.

"They must be dancing just for me," he replied, looking up at the sky and smiling absently. "Lucky, lucky me."

Chapter

Five

The drive home was quiet for a while, except for the faint sound of the radio.

Cormac could not get out of his head what Geegee had said he saw. What could it have been? A trick of the eyes … or the brain? And how do stars dance? He tried to imagine it but found it difficult.

"Do you have a favourite song?" Anele asked suddenly.

"I don't know," was his default answer to questions that were difficult for him to answer. "Do you?"

She nodded and pointed to the radio. "It's playing now," she giggled.

"Well, let's crank it up!" he chortled playfully and turned the volume up as loud as he could bear it to be.

He tried his best to guess the words and sing along, while making a big show of his hands and head movements. He wanted to make her laugh.

She put it softer and laughed, "It's *'clap'* not *'flap'*."

"Ooooh," Cormac drew the word out. "That makes much more sense."

He carried on playing the fool. Soon, she was laughing and even joined in the silliness. When the song ended, she put it softer again and put her hand on his leg. He shot her a quick look, then turned his attention back to the road. He could not help but smile.

"Thank you for today," she said at long last.

"I actually had a lot of fun," Cormac replied honestly. "Your parents are true characters."

Anele barked a laugh. "Try growing up with them," she snorted. She gave his leg a squeeze, and his smile glued itself to his face.

"Thank you for bringing me," he said.

She nodded and smiled, looking at him in a strange way.

"Do I have something on my face?" He added a gasp, like she had done the first time they had met.

She laughed again and shook her head. "No, you don't," she replied. After some time, she added, "It's just that I knew I had to bring you."

"Why is that?" he asked, frowning at her.

"My mother always said that the one I will want to bring home," she answered, looking quite serious, "will be the one for me, and she was right."

Cormac shot her a few glances, trying to figure out what she meant. As he approached a *robot*, the light turned red, so he slowed down and stopped. He turned towards her and tried to find the words.

"You ..." he tried, "you ... you ... you think that I'm the one for you?"

"I do," she answered so softly and so gently, he could feel the words caress his heart.

Her earnest face was pleading and vulnerable, yet she didn't seem anxious. He leaned towards her and took her face in his hands.

"I love you too," he whispered, and he slowly pulled her face towards his and gently kissed her.

Chapter

Six

There was nothing that could happen that would stop Cormac from smiling the following morning. Bright and early, Cormac stood in front of Anele's door and gave a spirited knock. He was holding a bunch of flowers he had gotten and a box of some strange yellow treats that Anele loved.

It was not Anele that opened the door though. It was Hanna.

"Good morning, Han," he greeted joyously. He pulled a white flower from the bunch and gave it to her.

"Oh, wow." Hanna seemed pleasantly surprised and gave him a small smile. "Thanks."

"I also brought some of those cakey things with the yellow filling that Anele likes so much," Cormac informed her proudly.

She waved him in and took the bouquet from him. "I'll put these into some water for you," she said, an earnest expression on her face, "and you better take those in to her. She'll need them." She added after a beat, "And you."

Cormac frowned. It was nice that Hanna had grown accustomed to him and that she had accepted him over the past months, but this didn't sound like the normal Hanna he had come to know.

"What's wrong?" he asked, looking at Anele's closed bedroom door.

"She got the call around five," Hanna said, filling a clear vase with water. "Her grandfather passed away during the night. She's been crying all morning."

Every muscle in his body went numb. Could it be possible? Had the man they had seen only a few hours ago ... died? He hadn't seen the man's colour, so he wouldn't have noticed a change in it. According to Inade, he wouldn't have been able to tell anyway until just before it happened. He had seemed so alive, so ready to start again with his new 'lady friend', as Riette had put it. How could it have ...

Cormac realised quickly that what he felt didn't mean anything now, actually; what mattered was Anele. She was the one in pain, hurting from the loss of her last grandparent. Gently, he knocked on her bedroom door and walked in. The curtains were still drawn, casting the room into a perpetual twilight. Anele was curled into a ball on her bed, facing the wall, tissues lying all around her on the bed and on the floor. She didn't look up as he walked in.

"I told you, Han," Anele wheezed, "I don't want to see anyone."

"I didn't realise I was anyone," Cormac mused as he sat down on the edge of her bed, setting the box of treats on the floor.

Anele whirled around when she heard his voice and seemed relieved. She threw her arms around his neck. Her body was shaking as she cried. "I can't believe it, Cormac!" she managed to say. "Geegee ... is ..."

"I know," he whispered and pulled her close.

They stayed like that a while as she cried. Cormac moved her onto his lap so that she would be more comfortable, handed her tissues as she needed them, and held her for as long as she needed.

Eventually, she moved off his lap and sat in the middle of the bed, legs crossed. She played with the tissue in her hand and dabbed at her eyes.

"I don't even remember if I told him—" she sniffed "— that I love him."

"I'm sure you did," Cormac said and reached down to pick up the box. "I brought you these," he whispered, laying it in front of her and opening the lid.

There was no joyful or delighted twinkle in her eyes when she saw the white-crusted yellow rectangles. All that her eyes did was look dark and red and sad. He hated seeing her like this, hated not being able to do more for her pain. Still, she picked one up, tissue still in hand, and ate it slowly. Completely off topic, Cormac suddenly wondered how she remained so thin while she ate so many treats and cakes and sweets.

After some time, Hanna brought them a pot of tea and then turned to Cormac, saying she had a very important job interview that she couldn't miss, and would he take care of Anele? *As if I have anywhere in any realm of existence that I would rather be,* he mused to himself. Still, he agreed, thanked her for the tea, and they were alone again.

It was not like before, not like the other times that they had been alone together. Then, there was a sense of excitement and longing to be with her and a sense of wonderment about her, mixed with worry that she would not feel the same for him when she found out the truth about him. Now, he only felt sadness and distress at her pain.

Anele's pain continued for a week, so Cormac only left her to get sustenance, fifteen minutes at a time every second day or so. He soon realised he didn't need it often. He slept next to her and held her through her painful nightmares that dripped with regret and sadness. He brought her food and drink, but she hardly touched anything. He did everything he could for her, but still, nothing seemed to ease her pain.

What kind of a world was this where people loved so deeply and hurt so much when their love was lost? It was driving Cormac mad. He wanted to make it stop. He wanted to change things. He wanted to make them better for Anele.

The funeral was a short one, as Geegee had requested it to be, so that people could get to the wake sooner. It turned out that Geegee's friends were a lively old bunch, and all they wanted to do was celebrate his life. Anele's large family was there too. It was awkward for him as he didn't know many people there, but he kept reminding himself that he was there for Anele, to support and comfort her. He now understood the conversation he overheard between Hanna and Nina at Joyce's husband's wake, about the awkwardness of not knowing anyone at a wake and the responsibility of making small talk.

Once they were back home and Anele was sound asleep, Cormac decided he would go back to HQ and find out what he could do to help stop Anele's hurting.

CHAPTER

SEVEN

CORMAC ARRIVED IN HQ by an elevator. He decided that was the best way to make it look like he didn't remember his ability to use doors as portals. He had been going into his room and coming out of it again. He hoped no one suspected that he was actually regularly leaving HQ. However, it was only as he stepped out of the elevator that he realised that he hadn't left through the elevator. No one gave him a second look though, so he hoped it would be okay.

As before, the foyer was filled with people coming this way and going that way. Some were still blurs but most had proper form. He looked around at the breathers that were there and their faces. No one was scared or seemed to be in pain. Everyone was smiling and talking happily amongst themselves. Cormac wondered if they were happy that they had transitioned or if it even mattered to them.

Standing on the opposite side of the foyer from him, in front of an out-going elevator, he saw someone he did not expect to see. Cormac made his way through the crowds of people, blurs and Guides and held out his hand as he greeted Geegee.

Geegee shook his hand firmly and smiled.

"You look well, Geegee," Cormac observed, slightly concerned. Geegee was standing up straight and didn't seem to have the same problems he had had with his knees.

"Lily here has been looking after me very well," he told Cormac happily. "She says that I'm going to be joining my beloved Bee."

Cormac had hardly noticed the woman standing next to Geegee. He started when he saw who it was. It was Orkid. It made a strange sort of sense though, when he thought about it: Orkid was Lily, and she had come into Geegee's life after his wife transitioned, to help *him* transition.

Orkid gave Cormac a wink. She greeted him fondly. "Good to see you again, Cormac." She giggled playfully.

"What are you hiding, devil woman?" Geegee chortled and grabbed Orkid's bottom.

She giggled again and smacked his hand away. "Oh, you little trickster," she chided.

Cormac frowned at the interaction. He wondered if Geegee truly understood what was happening to him, what *had* happened.

"Geegee?" Cormac asked. "Did Anele tell you she loved you when we left the other night?"

The old man seemed surprised by the question. "Of course she did," he replied. "She always does."

"Do you remember what happened to you?" Cormac asked softly.

Orkid gave Cormac a stern look, but he ignored it.

"You mean when I died?" Geegee asked. "I don't really. I went to sleep, and the next thing, my lovely Lily is there, telling me that everything is going to be all right and that she's there to take me to my Bee."

"No pain," Orkid said gently, "no memory of the moment. He's one of the lucky ones, really."

"When I saw the stars dancing for me," Geegee added, "I knew that it was my time. Tell my darling granddaughter that I love her very much and that she mustn't cry for me; she must live."

Cormac smiled, agreed, and said his farewells. As he walked away, he wished he could have brought Anele here to have that final conversation with him like she wanted to. Clearly, Geegee was happy and excited to move on so that he could be with his wife again.

When Cormac reached the entrance to the corridors that led to the rooms, he stopped and wondered where he should go and who he should speak to. Norrym would be far too doom and gloom and would have none of the answers that Cormac wanted. Jiëlle would more than likely try to take him to Ludis and, since Inade said not to bother him … A light bulb went on in his head: Inade.

He closed his eyes and pictured her colour. It led him straight to her. He opened his eyes and leaned forwards and let the invisible string pull him towards her. He kept his feet running so that he could try land properly this time.

It was only when he was outside the double-doors where Inade was that he realised he had travelled like he did in the Shade but inside HQ. Surely that wasn't right. And then he heard a voice in his head, an old voice, almost talking to itself, saying, *"Guides aren't meant to be in this realm and in the Shade."*

Cormac stumbled a step backwards. That was Ludis's voice! It was certainly Ludis, but he didn't remember seeing him before. Or did he? A shock hit him into the wall. He did remember! The memories flashed through his mind with such force he held onto the wall for support. He remembered looking for Inade and finding her talking with Ludis. He remembered how he had come out of the Shade and collapsed in Inade's arms … no, she pulled him out!

And it was her! She was the one that strapped him to that bed, and she … she and that other Guide … Hamnez? Yes! Hamnez. They poured something down his throat and forced him to drink it.

Cormac was breathing heavily, leaning hard against the wall. How could he have forgotten that? Norrym was right. They had taken the memories from him, but why? He had to get out of there, he had to leave before anyone—

Suddenly, flashes streaked across his mind: empty bottles, wooden flooring, the swinging door, high-fiving someone, a red dress, a car screeching towards him! Bam!

The door next to him opened, and voices came from within as Guides walked out. Cormac jumped away from the wall and tried to turn around and make as though he was walking away. He felt as though he could hardly stand as pain coursed through his whole body. He needed to get away, he needed to leave.

"Cormac?" It was Inade's voice. Of course it was. He had come here to find her, foolishly thinking that he could trust her. But he couldn't show it, couldn't think that he didn't anymore. He had to stay calm and breathe.

She took a step forwards and asked gently, "What are you doing here?"

"I uh …" he thought quickly, turning around and trying to smile at the group. "I came to see you." He decided to go with the truth, a part of it anyway, and tried to swallow away the shock of what he had just recalled and push it from his mind.

"Of course," she chimed with a friendly smile. "Let's go this way, shall we? I'll see you all later," she added to the other Guides, dismissing them with a wave of her hand.

They waved to her and walked away, while Cormac and Inade walked in the other direction.

"What is it you'd like to know?" she asked politely.

He had to keep his mind clear, had to keep her from realising that he remembered.

"I was wondering," he focused on his question, and then continued, "why do breathers have to die?"

Inade stopped walking and turned to face him. He stopped too.

"Why are you asking this, Cormac?" she enquired.

"When you and I talked in … in that strange room," he explained, "you said we do this to ensure the happiness of the human race. But I've seen what death does to the breathers, and it isn't happiness. So, why do we really do this?"

Inade looked up and down the corridor, then went to a door on her left. She opened it and invited Cormac in. It was a small room with only a small table and two chairs in it. Inade took the one and Cormac the other.

She sighed again. "It is true that the breathers are very sensitive about transitioning," she began. "It initially brings them pain and sadness, but it is not the ones that leave that feel this, only the ones that are left behind."

"I saw no sad faces in the foyer," Cormac commented.

"Exactly," she exclaimed. "The ones that are left behind are sad for their own loss, sad for the things they won't get to do again with their loved ones, and sad for the unspoken words. But eventually, that pain passes, and happiness continues."

"But *why* must anyone transition at all?" he reiterated.

Inade took a deep breath. "Guides aren't meant to know this," Inade warned, "but since you're asking, I will tell you. There is a delicate balance, Cormac, one that is appeased by the cyclical nature of the world. Breathers are born, given a certain amount of time to do with as they will, and when that time is over, they transition."

"And what happens if someone doesn't transition when they are supposed to?" he asked after a moment's thought.

"Then the balance is thrown off," Inade whispered, "and everything that holds the breathers' world in its cosy little bubble is destroyed." She sat up straight and waved her hand at the blank wall next to them. Images appeared on the wall, like they had before, of war and destruction and death. "When one person is favoured, this happens. Not always on this scale, but you get the idea."

"So, what you're saying is that if one person transitions before or after they are supposed to, the world falls into chaos?"

"Yes," she replied, "and it is up to us to set it right again."

The words echoed around his head, as he thanked her, as he walked back to the elevators, as he watched the doors close. That was what Ludis had said, that she had to 'set it right again'. As the doors closed, Cormac saw Inade running towards him, pale eyes wide with fear. He didn't stop the doors; he simply returned to Anele.

127

PART FOUR:

PERIL

CHAPTER

ONE

"HI HAN," CORMAC heard Anele say from the front door.

"Hey sweetie," Hanna's voice replied as the door closed. "You don't look ready."

"I know, I know. Sorry."

They walked into the lounge. Hanna smiled when she saw Cormac. "Hey Cormac," she said, putting her handbag and keys down. "Are you coming too?"

It had been two months since Geegee's passing and what Inade had said about the pain passing seemed to be true. Anele was becoming more herself again, smiling more, and the glimmer in her eyes was returning slowly.

Cormac looked up from the couch he was lying on. Erica had given him a book to read, so he was spending his days doing that. Confused by what Hanna had asked, he dropped the book onto his stomach and frowned at Anele. "Coming where?" he asked.

Hanna looked from Cormac to Anele. "While you tell him, I'm going to go shower," she said, then turned to leave. She stopped, looked back to Anele with meaning, and added, "We've got fifteen minutes before we need to leave, so be ready, Nelly!"

Cormac, feeling uncomfortable now, stood up and put the book onto the couch. He walked over to Anele. "What is she talking about?" he asked softly, taking hold of her hand.

"I'm sure I told you about our friend, Han's *special* friend, George," she elaborated as she walked into her bedroom, still holding his hand.

Cormac followed. "I'm sure you didn't."

"I'm sorry, beloved. This friend of ours, George, is throwing a big party tonight, and you have to come with!"

Cormac looked down at her cheeky, smiling face and could not help but smile back. Cormac strolled over to her desk chair and sat down. "Oh, do I?" he admonished.

She had turned towards her cupboard but froze when she heard his words. Slowly, she turned to face him. Her playful smile slowly disappeared, and she began to pout as she walked towards him. "Oh, pudding cup," she teased, slipping onto his lap and putting her arms around his neck. She kissed him on the cheek and then the forehead and then the nose.

Cormac's arms couldn't help but fold around her.

"Please will you come with me to George's party?" she asked, still feigning sadness.

Cormac laughed and kissed her neck. "Of course I will," he chortled as he picked her up and flung her onto the bed. He launched himself at her and began tickling her.

She laughed and laughed and thrashed about.

"Stop it, please!" she cried while she laughed breathlessly. "Please stop! Help! Help!"

Abruptly, Cormac stopped. He sat up. Another spark had just gone off in his brain.

"What is it?" Anele asked, putting her arms around his neck and kissing his cheek.

He put a hand on her arm. "What did you just say?" he asked quietly.

"I wasn't being serious," she assured. "It was just a joke."

"I know," he answered, frowning, "but what did you say?"

"I don't know." She let him go and sat next to him. "I said 'stop' and 'please help' or 'someone help'."

"'Help, help'," he repeated. "That's what you said."

The whole time his mind was whirling around, trying to place where this had happened before. It was a memory laced with fear ... fear for himself. In the room when he was strapped to the bed, he realised. He had shouted and kicked and tried to get away. He remembered now. He had begged for help, for Inade's help. But she had ignored his pleas. How could Inade have looked him in the eyes after having done something like that to him?

"What is it, Cormac?" Anele asked, stroking the side of his face.

Cormac softened his expression, looked at her and smiled. He shook his head and reassured her, "It's nothing."

He jumped to his feet, held out his hands for her to take, and pulled her to her feet, kissing her on the forehead. "Come on, you need to get ready," he announced. "You don't want to make Hanna late, do you?" He walked towards the door and smiled as he heard Anele laugh.

"Of course not!" she chuckled.

CHAPTER

TWO

CORMAC WAITED IN the lounge for the two to get ready.

He thought more about this feeling he had gotten. It was pure fear, one that made his heart race and made it difficult to breathe. He was amazed that one keyword, '*help*', seemed to trigger the memory. But when he repeated it to himself it didn't bring up any emotions. Maybe it was the way that Anele had yelled it? Unfortunately, it seemed more and more like Norrym was right and that he couldn't trust any of the Guides, especially not Inade. How could Inade have put him through that? And why?

It had been two weeks since he had returned to HQ to get some sustenance, and he knew he could probably do without it for a long time to come. So, he reasoned, he wouldn't have to see Inade for a while or Jiëlle or anyone from the Told. It would give him the space he thought he needed to get to the bottom of this ... this ... fear.

He didn't think about it for much longer. Soon, though longer than the fifteen minutes that Hanna had given them, the two were both pottering around the house, checking that they had everything. Finally, they were ready to go.

They went in Hanna's car and drove for about ten minutes. When they got to the right road, there were cars on both sides for quite a long way, but Hanna drove past them all and turned into the driveway to a house. In the paved area in front of the large house, there was a sign in front of one of the parking spaces that read 'HANNA'. She asked Cormac to move the sign for her, so he jumped out and did so.

Once the car was parked, Cormac replaced the sign. He frowned at it and asked, "Why do you have your own sign?"

"Because a certain *someone* wants to make Hanna feel special," Anele said and giggled from inside the car. Hanna's cheeks turned a vibrant red, and she hid her smile in her long, blonde hair.

Anele laughed and poked Hanna in the side.

The two women faffed around in the car, checking their purses and laughing.

"I thought we were in a hurry," Cormac said, looking puzzled.

They faffed for a little while longer, then got out of the car. As they headed towards the house, Anele took hold of Cormac's hand and gave him a big smile.

There were a lot of people streaming into the house, and Cormac could hear loud music and voices coming from inside. It looked like a huge party. As they entered through the large double doors, a tall, broad-shouldered blonde boy bounded over. He seemed nervous and fidgeted as he stood in front of them.

"Hey, George!" Anele greeted and reached up to hug him. "This is Cormac."

George shook his hand, mumbled something that Cormac didn't hear, and then looked back to Hanna. He had a grin stuck on his face.

"Let's go get a drink and leave those two awkward lovebirds to do their thing," Anele chuckled. She led him away. Cormac peered at them over his shoulder, at how stiff they both were, until they were out of sight.

The house was enormous. From what Cormac could see, there were at least three living areas downstairs and a grand staircase that led upstairs. There was a chain over the entrance to the staircase with a sign hanging from it that read 'NO ENTRY' but that didn't seem to stop some people from going up. At the end of the house, there was a square room with a small bar on the one wall and the opposite wall had sliding doors that stood open, leading to an outside area. Anele dragged him to the bar first.

The bar wasn't very busy, and the two guys behind it were chatting with some of the people that were there. Anele went to the side of the bar and called one of the bartenders over by name. She gave him a one-armed hug, chatted for a moment, and then he brought two bottles over. She thanked him and led Cormac through the doors to the outside. The whole time, she had not let go of his hand. A warmth spread through his body as he realised this, and not for the first time, he thought how perfectly her hand fitted into his.

Outside, there was a long pool, larger than the bar area, and beyond that a lush grass-covered hill that sloped upwards. There was a massive, bright spotlight that shone from above his head. He looked up and saw it was attached to the top of the house. Looking back to the garden, he could see groups of people sitting or standing on the lawn, everyone talking.

A large group of people began to wave at them. Anele, clearly recognising them, waved back, and they walked towards the group. On the way, she handed him one of the bottles she had gotten. He thanked her, and he took a sip. The taste was familiar; was this what he had had with Anele that first time they met? Was this the reason he had felt so ill? The coolness washed down his throat, and he stopped walking. Their interlinked hands jerked Anele back.

Her smile instantly faded. "What is it, Cormac?" she asked quickly.

"When we were at Papa Joe's, I had this?" he indicated the bottle.

"A beer? Hardly," she answered. "You only had a sip before you collapsed and threw it everywhere, and you started ... well, convulsing."

"Did I say anything when I woke up?" he asked earnestly.

"All you said was that you had to go to the bathroom," she replied, "and then you disappeared. Don't you remember?"

"I do," he said, coolly, "I just wanted to make sure that it didn't happen again." He took another sip and added, "See? I'm perfectly fine, so you don't have to worry about me."

Anele kissed him on the cheek. "Thanks, beloved," she smiled. "Can we go join my friends?"

He laughed and nodded. "Sure we can."

"Everyone," she called when they got to the waving group, "this is Cormac. Cormac, that's Dave, Junior, Lindi, Trevor, Pindie, Tamarin, and Sfiso."

Some of the faces in the group Cormac knew from the photos that were around the flat. They all cried a big hello to him and cheered and made a big fuss. They seemed a happy bunch of people. They made space for Anele and Cormac to sit down and not even then, Cormac realised, did Anele let go of his hand.

"Where's Hanna?" Lindi asked, looking around.

"With George, no doubt," Tamarin giggled, and the rest of the group laughed too.

Dave, a thin man with dark-framed glasses, tapped Cormac on the arm. "How'd you meet our Nelly?" he asked.

"Oh, uh …" Cormac was trying to find a way of answering the question which wouldn't give him away or sound awkward or weird.

"Through Hanna," Anele answered for him.

"Yes," Cormac said, smiling at her.

"Rad, man," Dave said.

"How do you know her?" Cormac asked, trying to be polite.

"We go way back," he said, "back to high school."

"Rad," Cormac tried. The word seemed clumsy on his tongue. He would not use it again.

Then someone said something about a Professor Lorenz, and everyone began talking about him. Cormac, not knowing this professor, watched Anele's group of friends. He liked seeing how she was with them, that she was the same excitable, energetic, playful person he had met at Joyce's birthday party and grown to love over these past months.

Now that he thought about it, it was the first time that he had thought about Joyce in a long time. She was his charge, the one he should be focused on, not out with a beautiful girl. What was he thinking?

Anele touched his arm and leaned closed to him. "What's wrong?" she asked.

Cormac looked up at her and smiled, looked into her stunning eyes, and knew the reason he was there. "Nothing can be wrong when I'm with you, my angel."

She smiled and rested her head on his shoulder.

"Thank you for coming with," she said. "Cheesy lines and all."

He kissed her on the top of her head, and said, "Of course." He ignored the rest of the group's noises and giggles. He didn't care what they thought, only that he loved Anele deeply and that she loved him.

From behind them, someone called her name. Anele spun around, saw who it was, and jumped up, grinning broadly. She ran to the man that made her smile, but it made Cormac's heart stop. *It can't be possible. Why would he be here?*

Anele walked over, still smiling, and looked at Cormac.

"Cormac," she said, "this is my very good friend of many years, Akael."

Cormac stood up, put on a tight smile, and held out his hand. "Good to meet you."

It didn't seem like Akael recognised him. He just shook Cormac's hand and smiled.

"Come join us, Kael," Anele invited excitedly.

"Relax, Nel. I'll come join you *just now*," Akael said. "First, I need to get something from my car. Cormac, wanna come help me?"

Cormac, seeing the encouraging look on Anele's face, nodded. "Sure."

"Great. Thanks, my man," Akael said and began to walk off.

Cormac kissed Anele on the hand and whispered, "I'll be back soon, okay? Don't go anywhere."

She nodded and smiled at him.

Cormac jogged to try catch up, but Akael was walking too quickly. Cormac resigned himself to following Akael from a distance. He followed him around the outside of the house and along a path. They reached a gate, and when it clicked open, Akael pushed it and held it while he waited for Cormac. By the dim light that was around them, Cormac could see that they were in a small courtyard with a stone table and two benches on either side.

"Is this where your car is?" Cormac asked tentatively.

"Don't be stupid, Cormac," Akael spat, "Guides don't use cars."

Clearly, the man had recognised him. It was clever of him, now that Cormac thought about it, to pretend that he didn't know him, just as he had pretended not to know Akael.

"Right," Cormac said at last. "So, what are you doing here?"

"What do you think, my man?" Akael asked. "She's my charge. What are *you* doing with *my* charge?"

Cormac ran a hand through his hair. This wasn't good. Did that mean that she would di—transition soon? How much time did he have with her?

"When?" he asked, frantically.

"What?"

"When?" Cormac repeated. "When will she transition?"

"What do you care? She isn't *your* charge."

Thinking quickly, Cormac retorted, "She is very close to my charge, and if she transitions before mine, that'll mean that I'll have to visit my charge another time. You see?"

Akael nodded, his face relaxing. He walked over to a bench and sat down, resting his arm on the table. "Yeah, I'm sorry, my man," he breathed. "Can't say I've ever bumped into another Guide out here."

Cormac joined him at the table. "Seriously?" Cormac breathed. "Never? It must happen sometimes."

Akael laughed a hearty laugh. "Of course, it does, it must. So, don't worry about it. I've not been with Told for long, you know. Can't say how long though. Longer than you, for sure."

Cormac forced a laugh, though he hoped it sounded more genuine to Akael than it did to his own ears. "Really?" he said. The idea that Guides had concepts of time seemed odd to Cormac. How could Akael tell how long he had been anywhere when Guides moved so freely in and out of time?

"Yeah," Akael answered with a smile. He seemed more at ease now, but Cormac was getting more and more worried. Akael's presence would complicate things. As much as he didn't want Anele knowing what he was, he sure didn't want Akael knowing about him and Anele. He would tell someone in HQ, and Cormac worried that what Norrym warned him about would be true: that they would steal his memories of Anele from him. Putting that out of his mind, Cormac probed again, "So, when is Anele meant to transition?"

"A week from now, her time," he answered. "Does that mess with your charge?"

"Yes," Cormac answered flatly, as it messed with him too. How could she transition when they had just found each other? Could he let her go? "When, exactly?"

"In the afternoon," Akael answered, "on Wednesday. I'm sorry, my man, but you know how these things work, hey?"

Cormac nodded. He still wasn't sure why they had to work this way though. Why did she *have to* go? Why couldn't she *stay* with him forever? All he knew for sure was that he wasn't about to ask *this* Guide for advice on this subject.

"Let's get back," Cormac said, after a moment's silence.

"Yeah, good idea."

While Akael was there, Cormac sat on the other side of the group. He didn't want him to guess at things that might look bad in the eyes of the Told. Holding hands would definitely look bad. He realised, as the night went on, that he was also hiding from Anele. How could he look at her when he knew that she had so little time left? Should he tell her? No, he couldn't. He would just have to save her. Inade had said that once marked, a breather's time was up and could not be changed. But there was something else that she had said too that sparked the beginnings of a plan within his mind. He knew that he would have to be careful, but he wouldn't let anything stop him from saving Anele.

CHAPTER

THREE

EACH DAY THAT passed, Cormac asked Anele what day it was. On Friday, they went to the movies in the evening with Hanna, Erica, and Aleiah. On Saturday, they helped Hanna clean the flat, then went to one of Hanna's friends' art show. On Sunday, they met with Hanna's sisters and Celeste at her bakery for tea. In the evening, he and Anele lay on the couch and watched TV. By Monday, Cormac felt like he couldn't keep such a big secret from her any longer. She went to visit a friend that needed help and left him behind. So, he paced the flat, thinking.

How was he going to tell her? Could he just say it? No, he would have to show her. But how much could he show her without letting other Guides know that he was trying to stop her transition from happening? Anele only returned late that evening, and still, Cormac could not bring himself to tell her the truth.

On Tuesday, Cormac begged her to spend the day with him and forget about her friend. She laughed and reminded him that that wasn't the sort of person she was. She told him not to worry and that everything would be fine. But he knew otherwise.

That night, Anele and Hanna decided to have a *braai* outside in the courtyard. Hanna cooked the meat on a warm fire, while Anele and Cormac chopped vegetables for a salad. The night air was warm, with a gentle breeze that jostled the smoke this way and that. The two women chatted as they always did, about important things and insignificant things. All the while, Cormac worried. After they had eaten and packed up, they carried everything back up the stairs to the flat. Halfway up the stairs, Anele stopped. Cormac, just behind her, was forced to stop too.

"What's wrong?" he asked.

She was staring into the sky, a far-off look on her face.

"Do you see it?" Anele whispered.

"See what?" Hanna asked from the top of the stairs, looking towards Anele.

Cormac stared at Anele; his heart had practically stopped.

"The stars ..." she breathed. Her eyes sparkled in their light.

"Yes, Nelly," Hanna said, turning and walking down the corridor to their flat, "the stars are out."

Cormac knew what she was going to say though, and it broke his heart, stole his breath, and glued his eyes to Anele.

"What do you see?" he managed at last.

Anele didn't look away from the sky and smiled serenely. "The stars ..." she repeated, "the stars are ... *dancing!*"

Cormac felt a dagger plunge deep into his chest, wrenching his breath from him. He grabbed hold of the railing for support.

Anele, breaking free from whatever magic had gripped her, put her hand out to Cormac. "What's wrong, beloved?"

Cormac was panting now. How? How was she seeing what Geegee had before he had died? Was this the sign? Was this the final confirmation that she would, for certain, die tomorrow? She couldn't! He wouldn't let her.

"Beloved?" Anele put her hand on Cormac's shoulder. "What's wrong?"

He wouldn't let her. This was all he knew and all he needed to know. He looked up at her beautiful face and attempted a smile. He shook his head and took another step up. "It's nothing," he groaned. "Just ate too much, I think."

Anele took his hand and led him up the stairs. She didn't look at the sky again, but Cormac could see on her face that she was remembering it.

Chapter

Four

Cormac did not sleep. He could not.

He lay there, next to Anele, trying to think how he could show her what he was in such a way that she wouldn't freak out or never speak to him again. When Anele woke, they had breakfast together, but she seemed to notice his mood and asked repeatedly if he was okay. What answer could he give that would make any sense?

He took their dishes to the kitchen and placed them next to the basin. When he came out, Anele was standing in the entrance hall, arms crossed, with a concerned expression on her face.

"Cormac," she said, leaning against the wall, "please talk to me."

Cormac closed his eyes and pictured Anele's face in his mind.

"What's wrong?" she asked. "Beloved. Please."

He didn't reply; he was concentrating. It was easy to draw her face in his mind. He had seen it so many times, traced its lines with his finger, kissed those lips. When he slowly opened his eyes, he saw, for the first time, Anele's colour. The light shone from every part of her, every eyelash, every inch of skin, and every fibre of clothing. It was brightest on her, but as it filled the room it shone a deep violet-red. The beams of coloured light flittered from and around her, like purple rays of sunlight moving through clouds.

"What is it?" she sounded alarmed now. Or was it apprehension? Her playful tone was gone, replaced by something akin to worry, but Cormac's smile didn't falter.

"Why are you looking at me like that?" she huffed. She was definitely feeling out of place.

Cormac slowly took a step towards her. Anele didn't move, her arms suddenly dropping to her sides. He took another step closer, feeling the warmth of her light wash over him. He took another step. He really was so in love with her, and he knew she loved him too. There was nothing that anyone could do that would change that. A last step, and he was right in front of her. She looked up at him, anxious but not afraid. He put his arms around her and hugged her tightly. He could feel her body tense at first, but then she relaxed, let out a sigh, and hugged him back. She lifted her head and looked at him.

"I love you," he said, seeing the violet light still dancing around her, "more than anything in this or any other world."

"I love you too," she replied and slowly raised herself up and pressed her lips against his.

Neither one saw that the violet-red light that came from her burst into an intense white light that exploded from the both of them. It was extraordinarily fierce and blazed for long after they pulled away from each other.

All they could see was each other.

Cormac took Anele's hand and led her to the couch.

"I have to tell you something," he said as he crouched in front of her, "and I want you to listen first, then ask questions, okay? Because I know you'll have questions, but I want to explain first. Is that all right?"

Anele was frowning, but she nodded. "Okay," she agreed.

And so Cormac began to explain: he explained what he was and how he found out; about waking up in the room; the images he saw in his head; the interaction between him and Jiëlle; going to Joyce's husband's funeral; the next meeting where he'd met her; all the things he'd learnt he could do, like the door transportation and using the Shade to travel; what he learnt his purpose was; and how he had moved away from his purpose because he loved her and wanted only to be with her. He also told her about the things he was beginning to remember, the things he had forgotten, like the seizure he had had with her; what he remembered seeing and feeling in the room where he had been strapped down; and how her word had brought the memory back to him completely, for he had only half remembered when he had been searching for Inade.

Total honesty. That's what he was going for now. There was no more hiding anything from her, there was no need to. She was about to die, so there was no point. Finally, he told her about the conversation he had had with Akael the night of George's party.

He probably rambled for a good few minutes, not pausing to think that he should not say something or put something differently.

All the while, Anele was quiet. Her forehead was set in a frown as she concentrated on what was being said. She didn't say anything and hardly moved the whole time that he spoke. He was unnerved by this, mostly because it was something he had never seen her do before.

Once he was done, he stood up and looked at her. She gave him the same look and said nothing.

"And that's the whole story," he said, feeling a little uncomfortable. "Yup, everything that has happened to me since I—"

"Can remember," Anele finished for him, her expression unchanged.

"Yes."

"And all of this is my fault," she concluded.

"What? No, no, no," Cormac waved his hands in front of him, "that's not it at all! I did what I did because I chose to, becau—"

"Because I'm so special, and you are so attracted to me, and you couldn't help yourself." Anele didn't seem happy at all.

"You're right," he began, "I couldn't help myself, but not for the reasons that you think." He knelt in front of her again and took both her hands in his, holding them tight. When she tried to pull them away, he held them tighter and stared at her. Finally, she looked him in the eyes, fiercely angry.

"It was your eyes," he said, gently stroking her hands with his thumbs, "your eyes that say everything about you. Your eyes pulled me in, Anele, and they have not let me go. I am truly, deeply in love with you. I am with you because of that and because you are my angel."

She was quiet for a moment, her angry forehead softened, but suddenly it came back, and she pulled her hands away. "So, this is still my fault," she huffed, standing up.

Cormac dropped hopelessly to the floor and sighed. "It is because of what I am," he sighed, "that I did what I did. Not because of you."

She made no reply.

"If I had told you what I was from the start," he asked gently, "would we have had any time together?"

Anele stepped over him, arms crossed, and walked around the room. "That's hardly the point, Cormac," she stressed. "You're dead! I've been dating a dead guy."

Cormac jumped to his feet and stood in front of her. He grabbed her hands and put them on his face. "Feel this," he commanded, dragging her hands across his cheeks.

"Do I feel dead? Do I sound dead? I'm not dead, Anele, I'm right here."

"That doesn't make it better," she stressed, trying to pull her hands away. "And you're also telling me that I'm going to die *to*day. What ... what am I supposed to do with that information? I don't know. Do you?"

"Let me save you!" he suggested excitedly.

"Let you?" she strained. A derisive laugh burst from her chest. "Let you ... Do you really think that you can find a way to prevent my fate?"

"Yes," Cormac said, "I have a plan."

Chapter

Five

Once Cormac had finished explaining his plan, Anele had more questions.

"But this is all going on the assumption that I *am* going to die, right?" Anele asked again. "But does Akael really know? I mean, for sure?"

They were standing in the kitchen while Cormac made coffee. "He must do," he replied, exasperated. He hated seeing her like this, hated being the cause of it. "He had no reason to lie to me."

"But how can you be sure?" she asked indignantly.

"I just am, Anele," he answered curtly.

"Cormac," she cried. "That's not good enough. This is my *life* we're talking about, not the outcome of some soccer game!"

Cormac threw the teaspoon down and leaned heavily against the counter, feeling his shoulder blades pulled with tension.

"Don't you think I know that?" he asked, his eyes closed. "Don't you think I care?"

"I know you do," she comforted, putting her hand on his shoulder, "but this plan is dangerous, and ... and ... I'm scared."

Cormac turned his face towards her and kissed her hand. "I know you are," he whispered. He straightened, turned towards Anele, and put his arms around her waist. He brushed a stray hair from her face and kissed her on the forehead. "I am too."

They stood holding each other for a moment, Cormac wanting so much for it never to end. It did though when Anele looked up at him again.

"Shall we do this then?" she asked.

Cormac kissed her head again and held her tight. "Yes," he replied softly.

CHAPTER

ANELE BROUGHT TWO backpacks into her room.

"Will these do?" she asked, holding them up for Cormac to see.

"Yes, they're perfect," Cormac answered, looking up from the clothing he had arranged on her bed.

"What's this?" Anele asked, putting the bags down and looking at the arrangement.

"Your disguise," he answered slyly. He picked up one of the bags and left the room, calling behind him, "Once you've put that on, put some clothes and anything you may need into the bag, okay?"

"Okay," Anele called absently after him.

He knew she was still staring at what he had chosen for her. He chuckled quietly to himself and headed into the kitchen. He began filling the bag with anything that he thought they may need. As he wasn't sure when they would be able to get food again, they would have to be prepared for anything.

Once he was done, Cormac walked back into Anele's room, closing the bag and slinging it onto his back. "Have you written that note to Han...na?" He trailed off when he saw Anele. She was wearing one of his extra coats over a long, flowing back top and black jeans. She looked beautiful and strange, looking so much like him it was eerie.

Anele gave a turn and posed. "How do I look?"

"Perfect!" he answered. "Letter, for Hanna? Is it done?"

Anele picked up a piece of paper from her desk, ran out of the room, then, seconds later, back in. "On her desk," Anele answered.

"Good. And are you all packed?"

Anele looked around for a moment, then nodded. "I think so."

"Anything you don't take now, you'll have to do without until we get settled, you know that?"

She said nothing, looking around again. She clicked her fingers, jumped towards her cupboard, scratched around, and pulled out a slim, long bag, which she stuffed into the top of her backpack, before tying it off.

She put the bag onto her back and, seeing Cormac's face, answered his unasked question, "First Aid Kit. Never know when it might come in handy."

Cormac nodded, smiled, and held out his hand. "All right," he said, "are we ready now?"

Anele looked at his hand and took hold of it, tighter than Cormac had expected. She took a deep breath and answered, "Yes."

They walked towards her bedroom door, which Cormac closed. He pulled it open again, and they stepped through. Anele gasped. They were not in her living room but in a dark bedroom that had a slightly musty smell to it. The moonlight that shone through the thin curtains showed a double bed next to them, an armchair in front of them, and a long vanity table next to the armchair.

"I believe you now," Anele whispered, squeezing Cormac's arm with her free hand.

He smiled down at her and gave her a reassuring squeeze back. "Could you please close the door?" he asked her, whispering too.

She turned and closed the door as softly as she could, while Cormac walked around the bed to the sleeping figure there. He saw a clock on the bedside table; it read 2:04 AM. They had clearly travelled in time, but Cormac didn't know how far forwards.

Gently, he placed a hand on the woman's shoulder and rubbed it, attempting to be soothing as she awoke.

The figure shrieked and backed away, as though waking from a nightmare.

"Joyce," Cormac whispered, "it's all right. It's just me."

Joyce patted down her hair. "Cormac?" she answered, squinting at him. "Is that you?" She reached for the bedside lamp.

Before her hand got to the table, Cormac took hold of it. "It's me, Joyce," Cormac calmed her. "It's time."

"But I'm in my nightgown."

Cormac could not help but laugh. "Don't worry about that," he answered with a smile. "Everything will be fine. Shall we go for our last walk?"

Joyce smiled up at him and slowly rolled the covers off of her legs. She gave Cormac a hand to help her out of bed. Anele ran forwards and took her other hand.

"Anele?" Joyce exclaimed.

"Hi Granny Joyce," Anele grinned.

"What are you doing here?" she asked, shock clear on her face.

"She's come to help you too," Cormac answered. He realised that there was a special way that his voice sounded when he spoke to Joyce, slightly lower than his normal voice and softer too.

Joyce nodded in acceptance of his answer and smiled. "I do always love seeing you, my dear," Joyce told Anele.

"I love seeing you too, Granny Joyce." Anele's voice was filled with warmth, but Cormac could see the worry on her face. "Shall we?" she added.

Cormac nodded.

Joyce linked her arms with the two youngsters, one into Cormac's and the other into Anele's, as they walked around the bed. Cormac didn't know what to expect, what would happen now. Would they have to walk through the door, him thinking about HQ? Or would there be another unexplained way that they would get there?

His questions were answered before they had even fully rounded the bed. The three were suddenly walking out of an elevator into the foyer at HQ.

It had worked! Anele was here and so was Joyce, and everything was working perfectly! They came out of an elevator towards the end of the line of elevators, far away from the front desk and the prying eyes of the Guides that were stationed there. Cormac led them towards an elevator straight ahead of them. There were two young people standing by the elevator that Cormac had chosen. He was hoping that they could stand with them for more cover.

Joyce asked Anele a question, but Cormac didn't hear what it was. As the two began to speak quietly, Cormac was looking around them, looking at the half-blurs and people around them. Would one of them somehow notice that Anele had not transitioned, that she should not be there? No one looked at them, or if they did it was because Cormac was looking at them.

Anele greeted the two boys, no older than eighteen, and asked them how they had gotten there.

The two looked at each other, then back to her.

"We were going home from Square," the one said.

Anele frowned. "But Square closed down years ago."

Cormac laughed awkwardly, trying to not get them to start asking questions. "Oh, never mind that," he chuckled.

The elevator in front of them slowly opened, and the two walked in, waving at them as they went.

"Should I go too?" Joyce asked.

"Hey!"

A loud voice shouted from across the foyer and echoed around the large space.

All eyes turned to the person who had shouted, including Anele, Joyce, and Cormac.

"Out of my way!" the voice shouted again.

Panic gripped Cormac's chest. It was Akael. He quickly turned to Joyce, took both her hands in his, and turned to face her.

"This was not how I wanted to do this, Joyce," he hurriedly said. "I wish you all the best. I am sure someone here will make sure you get to the right place. Ask for Orkid if you have any problems."

"What are you talking about, Cormac?" she asked, looking towards the shouting voice that was ploughing through the crowd towards them.

"We have to leave," Cormac urged. "Now."

He affectionately kissed Joyce on her hands, then let them go, ran for Anele, grabbed hers, and pulled them both into the Shade.

CHAPTER

SEVEN

AKAEL STORMED UP to Joyce, frantically waved his hands about, then stormed off towards the corridor that led towards the sleeping quarters, pushing a small boy over.

Cormac watched a tall man help the boy up but quickly looked to Anele when she squeezed his hand very tightly. "Can't they see us?" she whispered, half frantic.

"No," he answered, "Guides aren't even supposed to be able to do this."

"Is it all right that we do?" she squeaked.

"For a short time," he replied. He quickly gazed towards Akael. "Come on."

They followed Akael and his entourage of Guides down corridor after corridor and through a set of double doors into a large, muggy room with a high ceiling. From within the Shade, everything in the room looked dull, yet it felt as though this was how it truly was. There were tables tightly packed into the room, with papers appearing a short distance above each, then falling down slowly, while others lifted themselves up and disappeared. The grey winds of the Shade whirled around Cormac and Anele, as though trying to pull them away, but Cormac was determined. Knowing what Akael was going to do next would help him know how best to protect Anele.

So, they watched Akael. He moved through the maze of tables to the centre table. It was larger and higher than the rest and circular, with a walkway carved out of it for someone to stand in its centre. Akael strode up the walkway, laid his hands on the table, and it lit up for a second. Everything froze. Then, all the papers lifted into the air and disappeared. Even the Guides in the room stopped and looked at Akael.

"New plan," he called out, as new pages began to appear and disappear.

Guides positioned themselves around the outside of the central table and waited to receive pages from other Guides. Guides were grabbing pages, showing each other, discussing them, or flinging them back into the air. From what they could hear, they were not looking for him but for Anele.

She glanced up at him worriedly. He gave her hand a reassuring squeeze.

It wasn't strange for them not to be able to find him, after all, Inade had said he didn't have a colour. And for them not to be able to find Anele confirmed for him that the Guides could not track them while they were in the Shade.

"This is good," Cormac guaranteed.

"The girl has definitely vanished, Akael," Eddley confirmed, indicating the paper in front of her. She checked the paper again and added, "She was there, but then she was gone."

"When did she disappear from her own time stream?" Akael asked, not looking at Eddley.

"Two hours ago," she said.

"Send two to go check her last known location," he ordered.

Cormac got an idea. He winked at Anele and inclined his head towards Eddley.

Eddley spoke gruffly to two Guides, gave them a piece of paper, then returned to her own station. The two walked out the door and towards the elevators. Cormac and Anele jogged to get into the elevator before the two Guides and positioned themselves behind them. Listening to their conversation, which was only slightly muffled by the winds of the Shade, Cormac waited for the perfect moment.

One of the Guides, Enton, took the piece of paper out of his pocket. Cormac looked over his shoulder at it and saw the lines and swirls that danced on it. "She was last seen here," Enton said, pointing at a dot on a line where a curved line intersected it. "See how it criss-crosses here? Must have somehow changed something. We'll start there."

Cormac winked at Anele again, who glared at him irritably, then he put his face between the two Guides and whispered, "You've gone there and found no trace of her."

The elevator doors opened again, and they stepped out back into the foyer, discussing how they would tell Eddley that they didn't find anything. Anele clapped her hand over her mouth, muffling a shocked gasp.

"How did you do that?" she whispered very softly.

Cormac smiled. "I didn't know that worked on Guides too," he uttered, half to himself. Then, he was filled with excitement. "I'm going to carry on watching them, so I'm going to take you home, just for a few minutes. Okay?"

"No!" Anele hissed. "You can't leave me alone. They're looking for me."

"But they won't find you, my angel. I promise." He kissed her hard, grabbed her hand, and dragged her out of the elevator.

They were in her flat again.

"You'll be safe here," he promised again. "I'll be back real soon."

"No!" she shouted again, but he was gone before he heard her protest.

Part Five:

Flight

Chapter

One

"Are you sure this is correct?"

Akael glared at the Guide who had produced the page that he was brandishing about.

"I've double checked it," Illore said, a petite blonde Guide, smaller than Anele.

"I must see Ludis," Akael informed them. "Carry on. Eddley, take over."

This was what Cormac had been waiting for. From his vantage point within the Shade, he could safely follow them and hear all he needed to.

As Akael moved out from the table, the commotion stopped, and the lights dimmed, but everything came back once Eddley had stepped up and placed her hands as Akael had done. Akael stormed out of the room, page in hand, with Cormac hot on his heels. He went down the corridor, turned left and through a door, then up a flight of stairs and stopped at the top. He knocked on the door at the top of the stairs and waited, impatiently tapping the page between his fingers. It opened. He pushed it open faster than it was moving and walked through into another corridor.

The wall on their right-hand side was entirely made from glass. Through the glass, Cormac could see the foyer far below. He didn't have much time to think about it as Akael knocked on the door at the far end of the short corridor, and it opened like the previous one had. Cormac hurried to catch up.

The room that Akael walked into, Cormac had seen before. This was Ludis's office. He knew that the true colour of the walls was cream and that the carpet was actually red, but through the Shade, the colours blurred into greys and swam around. The winds of the Shade blew around Cormac stronger than before, pulling him towards the door. He shook his head at the wind, trying to tell it that he had to stay.

Inade and Ludis were both in the room, sitting on chairs by the desk. Ludis invited Akael to join them. Cormac kept his distance and merely listened. The last time he was here, he had his memories stolen; he would have to be more careful this time.

Akael placed the paper onto the table and pushed it towards Ludis.

Ludis picked it up and looked at it.

"Who is this for?" the older man asked as one hairy eyebrow rose.

"Cormac," Akael answered.

Ludis leaned forwards and handed the page to Inade. "What do you make of this?" he asked her.

She studied the page and, without looking up, answered, "Cormac isn't a threat."

"Is that what it tells you," he indicated the page with a tilt of his head, "or is that what you *feel?*"

Inade replaced the page on the desk and looked at Ludis. "Both."

"Then why does he have all of Told in an uproar?" he queried.

"Because they have not been told not to be concerned," she replied calmly. "Once they know not to, all will return to normal."

"But he's hidden my charge," Akael interjected.

"We all know that isn't possible, Akael," Inade refuted.

"Indeed, it is not," Ludis stared at Akael through narrowed eyes. "So, how then does a high-standing Guide such as yourself lose a charge?"

Akael shifted in his seat. "Look, my man." He flinched as Ludis glared at him. "Sorry, Ludis. It's not my fault. She's just gone. It was Cormac, I know it was. This shows that it was." Akael tapped the page indignantly.

"Whatever Cormac's involvement, Akael," Ludis reprimanded, standing up slowly and getting more and more irate, "she is *your* charge, and you do *not*, under any circumstances, distract other Guides from looking over their *own* charges!" By the end, he was shouting, a vein pulsing in his forehead.

Ludis straightened his jacket and stared at Akael. "Now," he hissed with a sickeningly rapturous smile, "go away, and tell everyone to *get back to work!*"

Akael shrank into his seat at Ludis's harsh words, then jumped to his feet, nodded and murmured his understanding, then left.

Ludis sat back down.

"What do you really think?" Ludis probed, touching the tips of his fingers together and peered over them at Inade, his tone even and dispassionate.

"I think that Cormac's true worth will be shown shortly," she answered nonchalantly.

"Damn your riddles, Azemik!" Ludis shouted, the vein pulsating on his forehead again as his hands came crashing down on the table. When he spoke again, it was through gritted teeth. "If he disturbs the balance, and we are left with another Afthol catastrophe, it will be on your head."

Inade, or Azemik, kept a calm pose. "He will be found, Ludis," she informed him, "and the balance won't be disturbed. He is one Guide, and she is one girl. It won't be the end of the world."

Cormac wondered what happened with Afthol and whether he was a Guide or a breather. Whatever happened must have been bad for it to be labelled a 'catastrophe'. Would him saving Anele lead to such a thing? But, on the other hand, could he let her go?

Inade spoke again. "I will take over the search, and I'll report back to you once I've found him," she assured him and headed towards the door.

"We can't let the balance be overthrown, Azemik," Ludis called after her. She merely waved over her shoulder and walked out of the room.

Cormac followed her. She walked through the corridor with the glass wall on one side. He had never seen the glass from inside the foyer, he thought as they walked past it. Perhaps it was concealed, as much was in this place.

She walked through the door, up a flight of stairs, and into another corridor. This one looked like all the others in HQ that he had seen: worn red carpet, yellow lights on the walls, but there were only three doors on one side of the corridor. Inade went to the first door that had the number 236 on it. The numbering in this place seemed totally random, Cormac realised as he checked the next door and saw that it was number 306.

Cormac followed her inside. It was much larger than his own room, with a larger bed, more floor space, a desk that completely covered the wall opposite the bed, and two chairs. Cormac was drawn to the desk and the wall above it, where pictures seemed to be a part of the wall, some large, some small, all overlapping one another. It covered a large section of the wall and had many people in them, smiling and looking happy. Their faces blurred in and out of focus as the winds blew over them.

"It reminds me of why we do what we do," Inade explained.

Cormac whirled around and stared at her. He was in the Shade! How could she know he was there?

"Because you're thinking loudly again, that's how," she answered his thought.

With a small turn, Cormac came out of the Shade.

"It's good to see you again," she admitted. "You certainly do get the trophy for the longest game of hide and seek ever played." She sat on the edge of her bed and began taking her shoes off.

"I'm not dangerous," Cormac said, deflated. He fingered a notch on the wooden table and didn't look at Inade.

"I know," she answered evenly.

"Then why is Akael acting like I am?"

Inade sighed. She stood up and pulled out a chair for him before sitting down on the other. "It's complicated, Cormac," she asserted.

"No, it's not," he scoffed, glaring at her. "It's very simple: I was brought here for reasons that aren't explained, to do a job that wasn't made clear, and something went wrong in my head, and now you want to punish me for my differences."

"Please, Cormac, sit," Inade urged.

"No, I won't! I've come here for one thing and one thing only: to save Anele's life."

Inade sighed.

"She isn't your charge, Cormac," Inade said softly.

"I don't care," he yelled, knocking the chair over. "It's not right that she should die."

"Neither is it right to keep her from her fate," she countered.

"It isn't right to steal my memories and keep the truth from me, yet you did that," he was incensed now. The thought of losing Anele after having found her what felt like seconds ago was too much to bear. "I won't let this happen, Inade. I won't!"

"You know about the memories," she nodded. "I suspected as much. How much do you remember?"

"I remember everything," he stressed. "Clearly you're not very good at doing the whole evil thing."

"I'm not evil, Cormac," Inade chuckled. Suddenly serious, she stood up and looked at him closely. "What has happened to you? You seem ... different."

"No, I'm not," he protested. "It's all of you. You were one way before, and then at the slightest sign of irregularity, you want to chop off my head!"

Inade snickered. "No one's going to chop your head off, Cormac."

"Don't laugh!" Cormac demanded.

"I'm sorry," she snickered again. "It's just that it's funny that you think that we'll harm you in any way."

"Oh, really?" he probed. "So, you strap me to a bed and make me forget about it. There's a good boy. No harm, no foul. Is that how it is?"

Inade's smile faltered. "Ah," she breathed, "well, that is a little harder to explain than I'd like."

"Try," he demanded in a bark.

"This is what I do, Cormac," she took a step towards him. "I am the Guardian of Memories, and you are so special, Cormac, don't you see it? You have changed! You have a colour now! It's impossible but you do! Can't you see it?"

"Don't change the subject," he spat. "Why did you take my memories?"

"You are completely impossible," she spoke with such glee it frightened Cormac. "You should never have woken up in that medical ward, you should never have remembered any of it, you should never have ... have ..." she studied him for a second and then continued with wonder in her voice and on her face, "have fallen ... in *love*. You truly are impossible. That's why I did what I did. I knew from the moment we met that you were different, Cormac, that you could save yourself."

Cormac shook his head. None of this made sense. "But ... why me?" he begged.

Inade inhaled to explain, but there was a knock on the door and a voice from the other side. "Hello?" It was Ludis.

Inade ran to him and grabbed his shoulders. "Run, Cormac," she whispered, an excitement in her voice that puzzled Cormac. "Run! As far as you can and keep her close! When you want to see me again, just call out 'Azemik', my true name."

The knock came again. "Azemik, are you there?" he called again.

"Now, run!"

She pushed him aside and walked towards the door. Before she pulled it open, Cormac had spun around and moved into the Shade.

Chapter

Two

Cormac appeared in Anele's flat.

She ran to him and flung her arms around him. "Cormac!" she breathed. "I'm so glad that you're back!" She hit him hard on the chest with a fist. "Don't you ever leave me alone again, okay!"

"Okay," he moaned, rubbing where she had hit him. "Did anyone come?" Cormac asked, trying to change the subject.

"No, they didn't," she answered crossly.

"Good," he breathed. He pulled her to him again and hugged her tightly. "Are you ready to go?" he asked.

There was a knock on the door and a familiar voice sounded, Akael's. "Nel," he called, "you home? Weren't we going to have lunch today?"

When she heard Akael's question, her face relaxed. "I … I think we were," she replied softly, as though in a dream.

Cormac grabbed her arms and gave her a gentle shake. "My angel," he whispered, "focus on me. We need to leave."

She shook her head and seemed to come out of it. She frowned as she grabbed her backpack and pulled it onto her back. "I don't know what happened," she whispered.

"It doesn't matter." Cormac gave her a kiss. "Now, let's go."

The knock came once more.

If Akael called again, they didn't hear because Cormac turned around and into the Shade, with Anele at his side.

Cormac looked at the blurring frame that was the door. Akael walked right through it.

"Where can we go?" Cormac asked quickly.

"My parents' house," she whispered, holding onto his hand so tightly he was certain it would leave an imprint.

Cormac closed his eyes, pictured it in his mind, and leaned forwards. They appeared in her parents' living room, the formal one where guests had tea, but they were in the Shade and unseen by her hazy parents who sat with a few other people there.

"Can they find us here?" Anele whispered, looking around, still in awe.

"I don't think so," he said, looking around.

Just then, two Guides walked through the entrance way into the lounge.

"They can't know we're here, can they?" she whispered frantically.

"I don't know," he answered, his tone matching her frightened one.

"Find Hanna," Anele suggested.

Again, Cormac closed his eyes, found Hanna, and leaned there.

There were also Guides with her, in the food court at their university, where Hanna was sitting and working.

"Pindie," Anele suggested.

His eyes closed, found Pindie, and went to her, but Guides were there as well.

"How do they know where we are going?" Anele asked anxiously.

Cormac thought quickly. "They don't," he answered and pulled her with him to somewhere where he was certain they would be safe.

They appeared in the room with the fireplace inside Papa Joe's. Cormac pulled her down behind a couch and took a deep breath.

"Why here?" she asked as they began to take off their backpacks.

"I wasn't found here the last time one of them was looking for me," he answered.

Anele put her backpack next to Cormac's and sat down on the grey, swirling floor. "How were they able to follow us, beloved?" she asked.

Breathing heavily, Cormac replied. "They must have sent people to each person that you know to see if they could find you like that," he answered and peered over the top of the couch. "One last attempt to find you."

Chapter

Three

"I can't ever go back, can I?"

There was a sad, almost resigned tone in Anele's voice. They had sat in silence for some time, listening to the winds whirl around them. Her eyes were downcast, and she didn't look at him. Cormac turned towards her and took her hands in his.

"I told you," he emphasised. "If you do, you *will* die."

Anele sighed and looked down again. "I know," she said, "but it's just ..."

"I know," he said. "Just think of it as our first holiday together. Just the two of us."

That made her smile. He loved to see her smile. He leaned forwards and kissed her.

Abruptly, the winds flung harsh gusts at them. It picked up their clothing, whirled around them, throwing the straps of their backpacks around.

"What's happening?" Anele asked, looking at Cormac in fright.

"I don't ... shh, listen!" Cormac's finger flew to his mouth.

They lowered themselves further behind the couch as the sound of voices travelled along the winds. At first, it was difficult to say whose voices they were, but as their words became clear, so did the speakers.

"... and we have ... find them ..." said the first, a female.

"... too difficult without knowing their colours ..." said the second, a male.

"... Ludis will end us if he knew we were here," said another, another male.

"We have to find her," said yet another.

Anele looked at Cormac and asked in a whisper, "Is that Akael?"

Cormac recognised the voice as well and nodded. He tapped his lips with his forefinger and listened closely.

The first spoke again. "But Ludis told you—" she began.

"The girl is *my* charge, and she is *my* responsibility," Akael interrupted, sounding more than a little irate. "If she doesn't transition ..." It almost sounded like a question.

"Ludis gave us strict instructions, gave *you* strict instructions," replied the second, who sounded a lot like Hamnez. "If we disobey him, it'll be a lot worse for us than for the world if she doesn't transition."

Anele gave Cormac a meaningful look. He could feel her eyes on him, but he had his eyes closed now, looking for Akael. When he found him, he saw that they were standing in a corridor back at HQ. They weren't anywhere close to them, which was a relief.

"So, how do we proceed?" asked the third who he could now see was Enton. He was looking at Akael. "Your charge, your orders."

Cormac didn't see anything more. Anele grabbed his arm and squeezed tightly. He looked at her questioning face.

"Let's get out of here," he suggested, picking up his backpack. He held out his hand to her, and they ran.

CHAPTER

FOUR

WHEN THEY ARRIVED at their first destination that Cormac had chosen, Anele lost her footing and almost fell. Cormac pulled her up by the hand he was still holding and caught her with the other.

"Jacobsdal?" Anele read the sign in front of them as Cormac helped her to stand up again. "Where the heck is Jacobsdal?"

"A little way down this road," Cormac said with a smile, his forehead hanging heavy over his eyes to shield them from the sun.

"And what are we to do here in Jacobsdal, pray tell?" she asked cynically.

"They've got a lovely winery and other farms, and lots of little things to offer," Cormac said, starting down the road. "We'll find something." He offered her a cheeky smile. As though giving in, Anele smiled too, shook her head, and ran to catch up with him.

The time they spent there was joyous. They saw the small town of Jacobsdal, met some lovely people, and did some farming, because, as Anele said, "why not." They even went to volunteer at the winery, which Cormac had read about. They did as much as they could there, but one night, about two weeks after they arrived, Anele ran into their room, panicked.

"They're here, Cormac," she whispered frantically, closing the door behind her as softly as she could. "They're here."

Immediately, Cormac jumped up from the mattress that lay on the ground and began throwing everything they had into their backpacks.

Voices outside were calling, but they couldn't hear what was said.

"Is that everything?" Cormac asked in a harsh whisper.

"I think so," she said, looking around.

"We can't leave a trace."

"I know!"

He had more than likely told her this a few times too many. But they really couldn't, the slightest suggestion that *they* were the ones that had been there and not some other random couple, they would be tracked down, and it would be game over for them. They would find a way, Cormac knew.

"Fine, let's go." Cormac held out his hand to her.

"No, wait," Anele whispered and ran into the en-suite bathroom.

"Anele, we don't have time for you to take a tinkle!" he stressed angrily.

The voices were getting closer and closer.

Cormac ran into the bathroom after her, both bags in hand. "What are you—" he stopped when he saw what she was doing. "Oh."

She was picking up all the toiletries that they had almost forgotten. Cormac threw one bag onto his back and held the other one open. He peered through the small window that looked onto the front of the house. Outside, there were people with torches walking down the road.

"They're almost here," he urged.

"There!" she whispered triumphantly and closed the bag. She pulled it onto her back and took Cormac's hand. They pulled through the familiar winds into the Shade and went to a new location.

Chapter

Five

Isandlwana Lodge was a beautiful place to stay in. There was initially some confusion as to who they were, but that was sorted out with a little trickery, thanks to the Shade. They stayed in the main lodge and tried everything at least twice, except the horse riding, which Cormac did not like. They were there for two weeks before they were found again.

So, they fled to a lovely spa in Aliwal North, which had natural hot springs. They only spent two days there as Anele wanted to go to Knysna. It seemed she was getting into the travelling and enjoying the adventuring that they were doing together. They stayed in Knysna for almost three weeks. Cormac was surprised at how much he enjoyed life there: it was beautiful, the people were friendly, the food was excellent wherever they went. And all the while, he had his angel with him.

Unfortunately, they were tracked down once again and off they went. They jumped around South Africa for longer than they could keep track of. They would spend a few days in some places and longer in others. It was a great way to see South Africa, Anele kept saying with a smile. Cormac would smile back, but it would fade quickly, a gnawing realisation in the back of his mind that this was no way for her to live. At some stage, they would have to face the Told and the Guides, no matter how much he didn't want that to happen.

Chapter

Six

It seemed that Anele was getting more and more comfortable with travelling through the Shade as time went on. She also seemed to be happy with the idea of avoiding her death.

After Zeerust, Anele wanted beaches again, so they went to St Lucia.

While there, the two were curled up on the couch one stormy evening, relaxing while Cormac flicked through the channels.

"Go back!" Anele asked.

Cormac duly did and asked, "What is it?"

"This," she answered and pointed to the news report, sitting up.

"... brings the death toll to thirty-seven within the Pretoria Central Area," the news presenter was saying. "Police are looking into the deaths of seven others in the surrounding areas to see if they are connected. Tshwane Metropolitan Chief of Police Xolani Ndlovu said, in her statement at the press conference yesterday, that all the deaths appear to be of natural causes and seem to be unrelated. However, doctors from Little Company of Mary Hospital and other institutions speculate that nature may not be the true cause. Stay tuned for more on this story as it unfolds.

"Now over to—"

Cormac changed the channel.

"Hey, I was watching that," Anele protested.

"And now we're watching this," he said. "A documentary about … uh, are those ducks?" He asked with a chuckle.

"Don't joke like that," Anele chastised, looking at him with a sadness and worry that made Cormac straighten up. "You don't think that that's because of …" she took a deep breath "… because of us, of me … Do you?"

Cormac studied her beautiful face. The lines of her forehead creased as she frowned, clearly worried about it. He had to console her.

"No, of course not," he responded quickly. "Why would you even say such a thing?"

"Well," she stopped and looked at the TV for support, "you said that Ludis said that if the balance is thrown off, then millions would die …"

He could not have such thoughts in her head. He couldn't let her doubt that they were doing the right thing. She was alive and that was what mattered.

"No …" he searched for the words, "what he said was that with this other guy, the balance was ruined, and millions died. He didn't say it would happen again."

"But don't you see, beloved," she stressed again, "I was meant to die months ago, and now other people are dying, for no apparent reason! Even the doctors are confused. They must be linked to me *somehow*. And it's even in Pretoria, my hometown, where we met and lived!"

"Oh, my angel," Cormac sighed and reached a hand to stroke her cheek.

Anele hit the hand away and stood up. "Don't 'oh, my angel' me, I'm serious."

Cormac stood up too. "And so am I," he said, with as much force as she had. "These deaths, and you and I are *not* related. I would know if they were."

"Really?" she asked, stepping back in what looked like surprise.

He stepped forwards, and with a straight face, he lied. "Really."

He reached out and took her face in his hands. He kissed it gently, trying to replace the memories of such bad things. Anele put her hands on his hips, and he sunk deep into her. He moved his hands down to her waist, then picked her up and carried her to the bedroom.

Chapter

Seven

More time passed, a few more places, and still the story about the rising death toll in Pretoria followed them wherever they went. It had spread to outlying areas too, Mamelodi, Centurion, Hartbeespoort, even Soshanguve and Hammanskraal had been affected. Families waking up one morning to find someone had died during the night, some had dropped dead while out at restaurants, some on their way to work. The more Cormac and Anele saw of this, the more uneasy Anele became, the less magic he saw in her eyes.

Cormac tried to get her mind off of it, but at every turn, she would find her way back to blaming herself.

They were in Port Nolloth, in a little bed and breakfast just off the beach, when they heard the news that there were now over one thousand dead in Pretoria and Johannesburg for no apparent reason and that many were now fleeing to escape the mysterious killing disease.

"I can't do this anymore, Cormac," she protested. This was clearly the last straw for her. "You know this is happening because I am still alive. I know you do. I can see it in your face."

Cormac grabbed Anele's hand and dragged her out of the very public reception area of the bed and breakfast, towards the beach.

"We can't keep running," she stressed. "More will die."

Once on the beach, Cormac cupped Anele's face in his hands. "Do you understand what you are asking me to do?"

She wrapped her fingers around his hands and squeezed her eyes closed. "I can't keep feeling this way," she wept.

He pulled her close to him and held her as he too began to weep. "I can't live any life without you," he managed through his tears.

"I'm so happy that I've had you in my life," her voice was muffled by his shirt, "even if it was only for a short while."

Cormac kissed the top of her head. "You will always be my all and everything, my angel."

There was only one thing to do now. As they stood, Cormac spun them into the Shade and to the best meeting place he could think of: the sandiest, most-deserted area he could find.

Part Six:

Surrender

Chapter

One

In the desert, Cormac and Anele made a fire. It was a big fire.

"Tom Hanks would be impressed," she said as they sat and watched the flames lick upwards to the darkened sky.

"Who's that?" he asked, confused.

"He's an actor. Now, there's another movie I never got to show you," she sighed, then the tears came, "and that I'll never watch again."

As Cormac held her, he wanted so much to change this plan. He didn't want to let her go, he wasn't ready, but how could he not let her do the right thing? *Easily*, it occurred to him. He got angry about it sometimes, about how willing she was to leave him alone in this world. How dare she? How dare she not want to be with him and stay alive? But as she cried, and he held her, he knew that she didn't. She just couldn't stand the weight of over a thousand lives on her conscience.

Once she had calmed, and he had too, he wiped the tears away and kissed her one last time.

"Are you ready, my angel?" he whispered.

She nodded her head and sat up.

"Azemik," he called to the night air. "Azemik! We are ready for you now."

Cormac closed his eyes and found Inade's colour. Soon, he saw her and that she was standing in the large room with all the tables and papers, where everyone had been looking for Anele and him before, surrounded by many Guides. She was talking to them, though he didn't know what she was saying. Her speech seeming to be completed, the Guides followed Inade out of the room. For a fraction of a second, Cormac thought that she looked at him, *at* him. Could she actually see him? She shook her head and walked on.

He felt Anele's hands on his arm. He opened his eyes and looked at her.

"What is it?" he asked but realised the question didn't need to be answered when he saw her scared face and where she was looking.

Beyond the fire, they could see a dozen or so Guides had arrived and, in front of them, stood Inade.

Cormac gave Anele's hand a squeeze and stood up. He pulled up his pants and corrected his jacket. He was going to take his time about this.

"Welcome all," Cormac said eventually.

The assembled stared at him; even Anele was giving him a funny look. He didn't really know what else to say. How could he say that the love of his life was prepared to give hers up to save the world?

"Well, I guess you all know why we are here," Cormac began.

"Because you are stupid?" Inade offered.

"What?" Cormac hissed. "You said—"

"I don't care what I said, Cormac," Inade interrupted, walking around the fire in a wide circle. "You had a good thing going here, you and your love, and now you want to throw it away just because she isn't okay with the repercussions?"

"Over a thousand people have died," Anele shouted, jumping to her feet. "Over a thousand families are mourning because I was selfish and wanted to live a little longer."

"No, Anele," Cormac pleaded, turning to her. He took her hands in his and kissed them. "It isn't your fault, my angel. It's mine. I was the selfish one."

"Ah," Inade sounded. Her piteous tone pulled both of their attentions to her, "so you're tired of being with *him* because he is selfish, is that it, my dear?"

Cormac didn't like the calculating smile on Inade's face. He couldn't understand what she was doing.

Anele pulled Cormac behind her and took a firm stance. "No," she cried, "I love him. I loved him from the moment I met him. I would spend the rest of all of time with him, if I could."

"If you could?" Inade repeated, that same smile on her face. "What makes you think you can't?"

"Stop playing with us, Inade," Cormac bellowed.

"Yes, Inade," a voice from the back of the Guides called. All eyes turned to the one who had spoken. Slowly, he walked through everyone and into the firelight. It was Norrym. "Don't toy with them."

"Norrym?" Cormac asked, honestly surprised to see him outside of the common room.

"Hello, Cormac," Norrym grinned, his balding head glistening in the flickering light. Norrym turned towards Inade and fixed her with an intense stare. "Inade, you shouldn't give them hope where there is none."

"Hope is what we give to everyone, Norrym," Inade smirked and crossed her arms, "you of all Guardians should know that."

Norrym laughed. It wasn't a pleasant sound, and it made Cormac feel uneasy. Or was his uneasiness coming from Inade calling Norrym a Guardian?

"Why did you call him that?" Cormac urged.

"None of your business," Norrym spat. He looked at Inade again, brow furrowed deeply. "Don't do this, Inade."

"I'm not doing anything," Inade answered. She walked towards Cormac and Anele and almost pleaded, "Cormac, why this girl?"

"She is everything to me," Cormac answered. He stood next to Anele and held her hand tightly, as though at any moment she might slip away. He looked down at her beautiful face and smiled. "I love the way she loves and trusts unconditionally; the way that she listens to your problems simply because she can; the way that she loves to eat sweet things and never gains any weight—" he chuckled and so did Anele "—and above all, the way that she, just by loving me, makes me feel complete. Everything that she is makes her my all and my everything."

Anele smiled up at him, tears welling up in her eyes. She rested her forehead against his chest and squeezed his hand.

Inade took a step closer. "There it is, Cormac," she said, excitement in her voice. "Don't you see it? She is your reason for existing, as you are hers. Don't you see yet how you can save yourselves?"

Anele wiped her face with her free hand and sniffed. She looked at Inade and asked simply, "But what about all those people who have died?"

"What about them?" Inade asked, exasperated.

"They are dead because of me," Anele squeaked. "Because of what we did."

"And nothing will change that," Norrym interjected again, walking closer.

Anele took a step back and squeezed Cormac's hand.

"Of course something can be done about that," Inade sneered. "Now, shut up, Norrym."

"Nothing will save those people," Norrym shouted. "Their deaths are on your heads—"

"Norrym ..." Inade glared at him.

"—their families' grief is at your feet—"

"Norrym ..." she dragged out his name menacingly.

"—and nothing you can do will ever make this right!"

Inade whirled around and flew at him, like a demented bird. She pinned him to the ground. The Guides tensed, some gasped and stumbled a step backwards.

"Stop this!" she shouted, holding his chin tightly so that his chubby cheeks peeled through her fingers. "You will not have them!"

"They will be *mine!*" Norrym hissed through gritted teeth.

"Caster, Hamnez," Inade called, looking up at the two Guides. "Take him back to the Told and put him in the medical ward."

The two Guides looked at each other, then did as they were told. They marched forwards and pulled the short man to his feet.

"Remember, Cormac," Norrym yelled as the two Guides tried to get a grip on him, "They lie to you. They will take her away from you!"

Cormac turned a little, putting one arm around Anele and pulling her tightly to him. "No," Cormac demanded, "they won't take her."

Norrym struggled, but the two larger men got a firm grip on him, whirled around, and disappeared.

"I won't let them take her," Cormac called again. "Norrym said you would take my memories like you took Jiëlle's happiness."

Jiëlle stepped into the firelight. "What are you talkin' about, Cormac?" she implored. "My happiness?"

Shielding Anele further with his own body, Cormac said, "Norrym told me that they changed you." He shot

Inade an accusing glance. "That they changed your memories like they changed mine and that's why you're not the happy person you were when you got there."

Jiëlle looked at Inade. She seemed to be searching for some response that would contradict what Cormac had said.

Inade shook her head. "We never did anything of the sort, Jiëlle," Inade sighed. She looked back to Cormac. "And I am sorry that you had to fall victim to Norrym's lies. If anything was done to Jiëlle, it was Norrym who did the doing."

"It doesn't matter," Cormac shouted. He felt Anele jump at his angry tone. He held her close and said more gently, "I won't let you take her."

"This is what I'm talking about, Cormac," Inade breathed, walking right up to them. "Your love and, in fact, all love is the most powerful thing in the world. It's more powerful than hate or loyalty or war. Love is what brings us together and helps us achieve what nothing else can. Love unites us and keeps the world spinning. Love, Cormac," she whispered now, "is something that no one can take away from us and is what we *always* remember."

Cormac looked at Inade with a frown. "What ... what are you talking about?"

"Don't you see it, Guides?" Inade called out, turning around and waving a hand. "Don't you see ... *their* colour?"

At these words, all eyes turned to the couple. They both tensed, holding tightly onto one another.

"What does she mean, beloved?" Anele whispered to Cormac, clutching his hand tighter.

"I don't know," he whispered back to her, not looking away from Inade.

Inade walked around the fire, gesticulating as she spoke. "For millennia, we have led you to believe that the colouring is an inanimate unresponsive marker, made to help us find them," she spoke loudly, looking at each

Guide one by one, "but, as is evidenced by them—" she stopped walking and pointed through the flames at Cormac and Anele "—colours have a life of their own. They are as much a living part of us as we are of them.

"Do you see it?" Inade looked the other Guides over, a self-satisfied smirk creasing her face.

Some hesitantly moved closer, staring at the two. For a moment, all was quiet, but slowly, looks of realisation began to pass through the group.

"How can that be?" one asked.

"It's not possible," said another.

"What are you talking about?" Cormac called across the flames.

"It's the most beautiful thing I've ever seen," from yet another.

"What is?" Cormac shouted. "What are you talking about? You said before that I have no colour, and I've seen Anele's: she has a purple colour."

The Guides, seeming to forget their mission, walked around either side of the fire and simply stared at the two of them.

A female Guide with blonde hair called Awteen stood closest to them and held out her hand. "It's warm," she said. She looked over her shoulder at the others and smiled broadly. "Can you feel it?"

"That's just the fire, Awteen," Cormac called.

Another Guide, Felwin, stopped next to Awteen. "No, she's right," he said. "I can feel the warmth too."

Others stepped closer too and agreed, some smiling. Inade was smiling too, and she turned on her heel and disappeared.

"It makes the fire seem cold," said another.

"It's impossible, though," Jiëlle uttered from the back of the group.

Inade reappeared with Ludis at her side. "Do you see?" she asked him.

Ludis's thin face was set in a hard expression, the firelight dancing unpleasantly across its lines. He said nothing but merely nodded.

"What is it?" Cormac shouted again. "What does it mean?"

"It's your colour, Cormac," Ludis announced. "The *two* of you have one colour." Ludis seemed to glide towards them, studying the two. "Can you not tell?" he asked.

"No," Cormac exhaled. When did this desperately bad conversation turn into this? He didn't want to drag it out any longer. He wanted to get this heartache over with. It was becoming too much for him to bear.

"Why do you think this has happened?" Ludis asked softly.

Cormac looked once more upon Anele's face, his heart feeling heavy. She was staring at the strange people around her, still clinging to him.

"It's because of her, isn't it?" Cormac asked, not looking away from her. "It's because of our feelings for each other." She looked at him and smiled. "Our love has pulled our colours together."

"Love unites us," Inade spoke, smiling, "in this life and the next."

All eyes now turned to Inade, confusion replacing the wonder from before.

"You mean to say ..." Ludis began.

"I don't mean to," Inade answered, "I *am* saying."

"And they found each other again?" Jiëlle enquired slowly. Then she gasped. "That's why he didn't have a colour before, why he had such a difficult transition, because he wasn't meant to leave yet!"

Anele looked up at Cormac again. "What do they mean?" she asked.

"A strong bond," Ludis began, walking towards them, "can bind people together for as long as the love is true—" He put a hand on each of their shoulders "—and love can bring them together again."

"But I didn't ..." Anele began, looking from Ludis to Cormac.

"You remember you told me about your best friend," Cormac began thoughtfully, "the one who died ..."

Anele gasped. Her hands flew to her open mouth. She looked to Cormac, then Inade, then Ludis. "Is he my JP?"

Cormac could hardly believe it himself.

Ludis took a step back and smiled. "Yes, he is."

Cormac looked to Anele again as she hugged him tightly. He wrapped his arms around her, and the memories came flooding back: the day in the park where they played on the swings, his birthday where they had gone out to celebrate, the courage he had almost found to tell Anele how he felt about her ... the accident. All the memories came back so quickly his legs buckled underneath him. He collapsed to the floor, still gripping Anele tightly.

"I always wanted to tell you," he was breathing heavily, "I always ... I always wanted to be the one that you called your own, but I never knew how to ..."

Anele pressed him to her. "You told me every day by just being there." Her voice cracked on the last word, but she still managed a smile. "I wanted to tell you too, but then that bar fight happened, and we got separated, and ... and ..."

"And you never got your chance," Ludis concluded for her. "Life as a breather is too short to waste on fear."

Anele pulled Cormac into a hug again and held him close to her chest.

Akael broke away from the group and addressed Ludis. "What do we do with them now?" he asked.

Ludis gave the Guide a questioning look.

"Thousands have transitioned and will continue to if we don't take her," Akael predicted.

Cormac hugged Anele closer to him. "No!" he shouted. "You can't take her."

"Akael is correct, Cormac," Ludis said. "We cannot let this continue."

All of the feelings that Cormac had – the fear of losing Anele, the joy in finding her properly, the impending emptiness without her – all came pouring out of his eyes as he frantically tried to think of a way to prevent it. "You can't," was all he could manage. "You can't."

Anele hugged him tighter.

"Take me instead," he offered, cheeks wet with regret. "Take me. Just let her live. She has so much to offer the world. Please," he begged, burying his face in her chest again, "please take me instead."

Anele knelt down and pulled his face away from her. "It'll be okay, beloved," she whispered, holding his face. "You will be okay without me."

Cormac couldn't breathe. He put a hand onto hers and cried, "You can't take her. Please!" he wept. "Please don't take her away from me. I've just found her again."

Anele began to cry as well. "Please don't cry, Cormac," she sobbed. "You're making this so hard."

"I won't survive without you," he admitted out loud for the first time. It felt like his heart exploded in his chest with grief and sadness. He couldn't exist without her; he knew that now. All the frustrations and doubts and worries that had built up in him over their time on the run came pouring out of him.

Anele held him close to her, stroking and kissing his head. "I will always be with you," she whispered. "I will always be a part of you."

Ludis crouched down next to them. "You know it is for the best," he whispered, "and then all will be set right again." Ludis looked at Inade, who nodded.

Anele glared at Ludis. "You need to promise me one thing," she commanded.

"Name it," Ludis agreed.

"You have to promise me that you will take care of him," she said, tears still falling from her face. "He is the best man I have ever known, and I've known him twice in my life. He deserves the best that any life can give him. Promise me you will take care of him."

"Consider it done."

Anele wrapped her arms around Cormac again and held him while they cried.

CHAPTER

TWO

THE GUIDES AND Guardians gathered around them.

"Take them."

It was Ludis that gave the command as he turned away.

Cormac looked up at Ludis, panicked, his tear-soaked face glistening in the dying firelight.

"You can't!" Anele shouted, holding Cormac closer to her. "You promised!"

Ludis did not turn around fully. He looked at the two over his shoulder and replied, "I promised to take care of him, and that is what I am doing." He inclined his head to the Guides, reiterating without words his command.

The Guides walked towards them. Cormac and Anele held tightly onto one another, still crying.

"You can't!" was all Cormac could say through his tears. "You can't! You can't!"

The Guides surrounded them and grabbed at them.

"No!" Anele shouted and elbowed one in the face, but there were too many.

They were pulled apart and pulled into the Shade within seconds. Ludis and Inade led them back to HQ.

"We need to correct their timeline first," Inade said to the Guides behind her.

"No!" Anele shouted, struggling against the hands that held her. "Let him go!"

"Please," Cormac cried, "you can't!"

They appeared in the Told HQ by elevator. The foyer was brim-full with people, but they were all frozen in half acted-out positions. Cormac and Anele grabbed at the people they passed and grabbed for each other, still fighting to get back to one another. The Guides pulled them onwards and followed Ludis and Inade through the unmoving breathers and Guides in the foyer and into a corridor. All the while, Cormac and Anele cried out to be released and told each other how much they loved one another.

Their cries were ignored.

They were taken through a large set of double doors that swung inwards, into a room with many curtains on either side. Cormac's heart began to race faster. "No!" he shouted. "No! You can't do this! You can't take her from me again!"

They were taken into separate curtained areas. Cormac could hear Anele shouting at the Guides to let her go, let him go, then she called out to him. "Cormac!" she shouted.

"My angel!" he called back.

"Always remember—" She groaned, sounding like she was struggling against being fastened down. "Always remember that I love you more than anything in this or any other world."

Her words resonated with Cormac. He remembered having said them to her what felt like an age ago. He was strapped to a bed now too, two Guides checking the straps and a third standing back. There was a noise that Cormac almost heard, and the third opened the curtains. Ludis walked in.

"Did you get it?" he asked the third.

The third shook his head and replied. "Awteen has gone to retrieve it."

Ludis nodded and walked out again.

Cormac had no more energy to fight them, so he called out, "My angel? You remember that day in the park?"

He heard Anele shout profanities at some of the Guides, then she replied, "On the swings?"

"Yes."

"It was the day—" she cursed again, and Cormac thought he heard her spit "—the day I almost told you how I felt."

"I wanted to tell you that day too," Cormac sobbed. "I wanted to tell you that you meant the world to me. That, that having you in my life made even the darkest of times seem bright. You have made everything bright, Anele," he was openly crying again, "and I will always remember you."

CHAPTER

THREE

LUDIS RETURNED MOMENTS later.

"What did you do to Anele?" Cormac demanded. He could no longer hear Anele, and she was not responding to his calls. He had found some strength, he realised, as he thrashed about under the restraints. "Tell me!"

Ludis waved a hand at the two Guides standing by. They swooped down on Cormac and held him down.

"Just tell me!" Cormac demanded, still trying, in vain, to get free. "If you're going to kill me too, you might as well tell me."

Ludis stopped and gave Cormac a puzzled look. "I promised to look after you, Cormac," he muttered, "so why would I kill you?"

"Why did you kill *her*?!"

Ludis said nothing more. He made his way slowly around the bed, with something in his hands. He was carrying the box from Cormac's locker, he recognised it instantly. As Ludis approached him, Cormac tried as much as he could to inch away. It was no use though; the two Guides and the straps were holding him so tightly.

"No!" Cormac shouted. "No! Please! Just tell me what happened to Anele!"

Ludis still said nothing. He delicately opened the box. He stood next to Cormac's head, exactly where Inade had stood when he was last strapped to a bed like this. The fear gripped him, as it had gripped him before, and he tried to kick his restraints off, tried to shake himself loose, tried to break free. Ludis put his long, gaunt hand into the box and clenched whatever was inside.

"No!" Cormac called out again. He looked at the Guide on his other side. "Please!" he pleaded. "Please help me!"

Leaning forwards, Ludis placed his clenched hand on Cormac's forehead.

"Please!" Cormac begged. "Please don't."

A light shone out of Ludis's hand as he slowly put his hand on Cormac's forehead and began to open it. The light drilled into Cormac's head, sending sharp, teeth-gritting, nails-on-chalkboard pain searing into his head. Cormac shouted out in agony, but the more he shouted and writhed and squirmed, the more Ludis pressed the handful of light into his forehead. The anguish was unbearable! Cormac couldn't feel his legs or his arms anymore. All he felt was the relentless, rigorous, ruthless drilling into his head, his mind, his being. It was too much!

The last thought that went through Cormac's mind was a wish that Anele had not gone through this pain too.

And then everything went black.

PART SEVEN:

RELIEVED

CHAPTER

ONE

EVEN THOUGH HIS eyes were open, it was pitch black. Whether his eyes were open or closed seemed to make no difference. He tested the darkness a few times but still found that it was utterly black. He let out a sigh and tried to focus on other things. What could he tell for certain? He knew that he was lying on his back on a soft surface, what he thought could be a mattress. He prodded it with his hands, and it definitely felt like a mattress.

As he sat up, a groan emanated from next to him. He felt for where it had come from and realised that there was someone next to him. There were no other noises, he noticed with a frown. He swung his legs over the edge of the mattress and felt the carpeted floor below his feet. He also saw a thin sliver of warm light creeping in from under what he assumed was a door far across the black space. The light was just enough for him to make out the outline of a bedside table and a lamp on top of it. He fumbled around, looking for the switch and, when he eventually found it, turned on the light.

When his eyes had adjusted to the soft light, he looked down and saw that he was wearing only a pair of sleeping shorts. It occurred to him that he had no recollection of this item of clothing or ever having put it on. Or did he? There was a niggle in the back of his mind that suggested that he might remember something about it. He frowned and looked around for some sort of clue as to what was going on. He knew the room he was in, but he didn't remember how he had gotten there. He looked upon the person next to him, and he realised, with a soft smile, that he knew her too. It was Anele.

He rubbed his face, trying to shake off the feeling that he had been somewhere else, somewhere very far away.

"Beloved?" Anele groaned, rolling over to face him.

He lay down next to her again and gently brushed the hair from her face. "Yes, my angel?" he asked softly.

"Why is the light on?" she asked, opening one of her beautiful eyes only a crack.

"I ... uh ..." he stumbled, unsure of what to say. He lay on his back and put a hand behind his head. "I woke up and ... I don't know ... I ..."

Anele pushed herself up onto her elbow, eyes suddenly wide. "We're in my room," she observed, panicked.

"I know," he said, looking around the room too, less surprised than she was.

"But we were ..." she began, blinking the sleep from her eyes, "... were ..."

"In the desert," he said.

"And many people had died."

"And your death was the only way to stop it."

"And you wouldn't let me go." She smiled and kissed his forehead.

"Was it a dream?" he asked.

"That we both had?" she pointed out. "I don't think so."

He was quiet for a moment, then he rolled his head to the side to look at her. "So ... then ... that did happen?" he asked. "Was I really dead and were you really going to give yourself up to save those people?"

Anele looked confused but nodded. "I guess so."

"Then, why are we in your bedroom?"

All at once, it came back to them: the promise from Ludis, them being taken to HQ, the beds they were strapped into.

"I remember the tall woman," Anele said, looking around the room, "you called her Inade? She poured something into my mouth."

"Did it burn?" he worried that Inade had given her the same charcoal stuff that had made him forget.

"No," Anele answered distantly, "it was sweet, almost like honey ..." She turned back to him with purpose. "And what did they do to you?"

"I'm not sure," he admitted, pushing himself up, "but it hurt." He stood up and looked around for a moment.

"Where are you going?" she asked, panicked.

He held out a hand, "Let's go look outside."

Anele nodded and took his hand.

When they walked out of the room, they were in the living room of her and Hanna's flat, just as they had left it the day they ran. They could hear Hanna breathing heavily as she slept in her room, her door standing open. The clock on the wall read three minutes to seven o'clock. Still holding each other's hands, they walked to the front door. As they peered through the gate beyond the door, they could see that the sun was shining brightly, and they could hear the birds chirping.

"What day is it?" Anele asked absently.

He looked along the corridor and saw a newspaper lying on the floor a few doors down. He ran and picked it up to show her.

"It's the day we left," she gasped. "The day I was supposed to die! But what does it mean?"

He stared at the date. "They must have put us back," he breathed.

"After they 'fixed our timelines'?" she quoted with her index and second fingers waggling the quotation marks in the air. "Whatever that means."

"Must have."

"But what does that *mean*?" she emphasised, squeezing his hand.

He smiled and wrapped his arms around her. She hugged him back. He kissed her on the head and whispered, "It means we have a second chance."

The Final

Hidden in the Shade, Inade and Ludis stood and watched the couple.

"We did the right thing," Inade said, smiling happily.

"Did we?" Ludis was frowning.

"Those who weren't supposed to transition didn't," Inade began, "including him. And the balance has been restored. I definitely think we did the right thing."

"But she was meant to." Ludis pointed at Anele.

"Had he not died, she wouldn't have either, simple as that." Inade was very chuffed with herself.

"And you always have an answer for everything," Ludis chuckled. It would have been an odd sound to those who heard it.

"Always," she chortled.

He frowned, then asked, "What of ... what did the youngsters call him, Norrym?"

Inade smiled serenely. "He has been dealt with," she replied. "He will *not* be upsetting any more Guides."

"And so, the True Order has been restored." Ludis too seemed proud of what they had accomplished.

WHEN THE STARS DANCE

GLOSSARY

OF TERMS

Below is a list of South African terms that are used in this story.

braai – the South African term for a barbeque

hallo – hello

just now – the immediate future, or perhaps some time after that; later on

(*my*) *moeder* – (my) mother

hy's mooi – he's nice/good looking

my liefste – term of endearment, meaning 'my dearest'

robot – a term for a traffic light

tannie – aunty/respectful term for an older woman

Tuks – the nickname for the University of Pretoria

baba – father

ABOUT THE

AUTHOR

Hi! Robyn here. If you don't know, I am an indie author and language editor from South Africa. I live to write, talk, eat and visit with friends, and garden, but top of that list is write!

The decent ideas come from any random thoughts that may wonder through my mind, or from a dream, or even from a music video or quote.

The point of all of my stories is not only to entertain but also to show that things aren't as bad as they seem or that, hey, it could be a whole lot worse.

I write in the genres of fantasy and science fiction, and a whole lot in between, but the stories take on a myriad of forms, deal with a variety of issues, and the hope is always that they please and satisfy.

I deeply hope that you have enjoyed this book! If you did, or even if you didn't, let me know in any of these places:

https://www.facebook.com/AuthorRobynAnakinVeary/

https://www.instagram.com/authorrobynanakinveary/

https://www.pinterest.com/authorrobynanakinveary/

https://twitter.com/AuthorRAV/

Go to robynanakinveary.com to find out more about me. You can also check out my blog and newsletter there:

https://robynanakinveary.com/blog/

https://robynanakinveary.com/newsletter

www.ingramcontent.com/pod-product-compliance
Lightning Source LLC
Chambersburg PA
CBHW030741110726
47900CB00008B/2400